THE FALCONER'S

APPRENTICE

Malve von Hassell

"Sonnet: On the Fitness of Seasons," translated by Dante Gabriel Rossetti, attributed to Enzio, king of Sardinia, and derived from Ecclesiastes 3:1, on page vii, appeared in Dante Gabriel Rossetti, *Dante and his Circle: With the Italian Poets Preceding Him (1100-1200-1300),* Dante Gabriel Rossetti, Boston: Roberts Brothers, 1887, page 186.

The subtitles and quotes on pages xi, 21, 49, 77, 99, 129, 159, and 185 are from Frederick von Hohenstaufen, *The Art of Falconry: Being the De Arte Venandi cum Avibus*, translated and edited by Casey A. Wood and F. Marjorie Fyfe. Stanford: Stanford University Press, 1943, pages 6, 128–129, 130, 150, 151, 216, 365, and 391.

The excerpts from the poems by King Enzio were translated from the Italian by Malve von Hassell. For the poems on pages 151 and 158, she used the source text, Giovanni Pascoli, *Poemi italici e canzoni di Re Enzio*, IV Edizione, Bologna, Italy: Nicola Zanichelli editore, 1928, pages 54 and 63; for the poem on page 202, she used the source text, Bruno Panvini, La scuola poetica siciliana: *le canzoni dei rimatori nativi di Sicilia*, Florence, Italy: L. S. Olschki, 1955, page 173.

Library of Congress Control Number: 2014945791

ISBN 978-1-7371011-9-2 (hardcover)
ISBN 978-1-7371011-8-5 (paperback)
(ebook)

To my brother

Adrian von Hassell
1956–2009

Sonnet: *On the Fitness of Seasons* by Enzio, king of

Sardinia Translated by Dante Gabriel Rossetti

There is a time to mount; to humble thee
A time; a time to talk, and hold thy peace;
A time to labor, and a time to cease;
A time to take thy measures patiently;
A time to watch what Time's next step may be;
A time to make light count of menaces,
And to think over them a time there is;
There is a time when to seem not to see.
Wherefore I hold him well-advised and sage
Who evermore keeps prudence facing him,
And lets his life slide with occasion;
And so comports himself, through youth to age,
That never any man at any time
Can say, Not thus, but thus thou shouldst have done.

TABLE OF CONTENTS

Part I

Castle Kragenberg – *On the Instruction and Training of Falcons and Falconers*

Chapter 1.. 11
Chapter 2.. 18
Chapter 3.. 22
Chapter 4.. 26

Part II

Uncertain Sanctuary – *On Calling a Peregrine to the Lure*

Chapter 5.. 33
Chapter 6.. 41
Chapter 7.. 45
Chapter 8.. 49

Part III

On the Road – *On Transporting Falcons through Various Regions*

Chapter 9.. 59
Chapter 10.. 64
Chapter 11.. 70
Chapter 12.. 75

Part IV

Over the Mountains – *On the Improper Handling of Falcons*

Chapter 13.. 85
Chapter 14.. 89
Chapter 15.. 95
Chapter 16.. 100

Part V
Moving South – *How to Capture a Falcon*

Chapter 17.. 107
Chapter 18.. 113
Chapter 19.. 117
Chapter 20.. 125

Part VI
King Enzio – *On the Proper Care of a Falcon in Captivity*

Chapter 21.. 135
Chapter 22.. 141
Chapter 23.. 147
Chapter 24.. 156

Part VII
Castle on a Hill – *Lessons in the Proper Aims and
Qualifications of the True Falconer*

Chapter 25.. 163
Chapter 26.. 169
Chapter 27.. 176
Chapter 28.. 180

Part VIII
Partings and Beginnings – *Retrieving a Nomadic Falcon*

Chapter 29.. 189
Chapter 30.. 193
Chapter 31.. 197
Chapter 32.. 201

Epilogue.. 205
Notes to reader..208
Acknowledgements..212
About the Book.. 213
About the Author..214

PART I

CASTLE KRAGENBERG

On the Instruction and Training of Falcons and Falconers

"Falcons and other hawks are rendered clumsy or entirely unmanageable if placed under control of an ignorant interloper. By using his hearing and eyesight alone an ignoramus may learn something about other kinds of hunting in a short time; but without an experienced teacher and frequent exercise of the art properly directed no one, noble or ignoble, can hope to gain in a short time an expert or even an ordinary knowledge of falconry."
- Frederick von Hohenstaufen, *The Art of Falconry: Being the De Arte Venandi cum Avibus of Frederick II of Hohenstaufen*

Chapter 1

"THAT BIRD SHOULD BE DESTROYED!"

Andreas stared at Ethelbert in shock. Blood from an angry-looking gash on the young lord's cheek dripped onto his embroidered tunic. Andreas clutched the handles of the basket containing the young peregrine. Perhaps this was a dream—if he blinked, he would wake up in the boys' dormitory.

The night before, Andreas had not been able to sleep for a long time. Oswald, the head falconer at Castle Kragenberg, had asked Andreas to help during the hunt. Until that April morning, Andreas had never been allowed to go along when a hunt party set out. He always stayed behind, cleaning around the perches, sorting hunting equipment, and doing his other chores. Maybe a visiting lord would be so impressed by his skills that he would make Andreas falconer in his mews. Andreas smiled ruefully as he lay on his pallet in the dark and stuffy dormitory. The chances of something like this happening were about as great as Andreas getting to fly a gyrfalcon, the falcon of emperors.

Andreas woke up at first light, filled with anticipation. The other boys with whom he shared the dormitory were still asleep. Quickly, he pulled on his tunic and splashed water on his face from the little basin in the corner. When he got down to the kitchen, Matilda was already at her post, getting the fire going and filling large pots with water. Her solid bulk exuded energy and warmth.

"What are you doing up so early?" she asked. "I am supposed to help Oswald today."

"Well, eat something before you go." Matilda placed a wooden bowl filled with gruel on the table. A puddle of honey melted in the center of the steaming oatmeal. Occasionally glancing at Andreas as he ate, Matilda rolled out dough, pushing it and folding it over again and again in a smooth rhythm. Ever since Andreas had first come to live in the castle as an eight-year-old boy, lost and desolate after his mother's death, Matilda had taken care of him, fussing and scolding as if he were her son.

Finally, Andreas scraped his bowl and got up. He took it over to the scullery. "I will be back in the afternoon." He smiled at her.

Matilda's face, reddened and rough from years of work in the castle kitchen and accustomed to an expression of severity, struggled into a responding smile. She reached up as if to stroke his arm, but then her gesture turned into an abrupt pat. "Get on with you! Don't get back too late, or there will be trouble."

In the mews, Oswald was setting out the equipment and baskets needed for the hunt. "It's about time you got here!" he said grumpily.

"Good morning to you, too!" Andreas had lost his fear of Oswald a long time ago. Oswald was like a grandfather to Andreas, a stern mentor, and the purveyor of endless stories about worlds far away from the drafty rooms of Castle Kragenberg. "How is the merlin doing?"

"Go see for yourself."

Yesterday, on his way back from the woods, carrying a basket filled with dandelion flowers and young nettle leaves for Matilda, he had encountered four boys from the village bent on torturing the young merlin. The bird was on the ground, unable to fly away. Its jesses had gotten entangled in a branch. These thin leather straps, attached to a hunting bird's feet, were used to secure the bird on its perch and to make retrieval easier, but they could entrap a bird lost in the woods.

Normally, Andreas avoided these boys. He was afraid of them; besides, if he fought back, he might end up getting punished by the castellan. But yesterday, when Andreas saw them pelting the bird with stones, he was enraged and threw all caution to the wind. Armed with a stick, he raced toward the boys, yelling as loudly as he could. To his surprise, when they saw Andreas, they fled. Elated by his success, Andreas carefully picked up the injured young bird, wrapped it into his jerkin, and brought it back to the mews.

This morning, the merlin looked content and apparently recovered from the shock of being attacked. Its eyes were bright, and it did not seem to be afraid. Other than the crusted spot where a stone had hit the bird, Andreas could not see anything wrong with it.

Oswald said, "Lady Bertha is sending someone over later to pick it up."

Andreas nodded. He liked Lady Bertha, a widowed cousin of Count Cuno. Tough but fair-minded and generous, she governed her neighboring estate with a firm hand, keeping it intact for her eldest son.

"She was very grateful. But, Andreas, I did not tell her any details of who had found the merlin or how it got hurt, because I did not want to make more trouble for you with the other boys."

Andreas did not say anything. He kept his eyes on the merlin. The village boys hated him for living in the castle. "You think you are so fine! You are just an upstart!" they jeered. "I bet it wasn't your mother's needlework that got you into the castle!"

It did not help that the pages and Count Cuno's sons, with whom Andreas attended lessons, also despised him and considered him as little more than a cadger. Brother Stefan, the tutor, had done what he could to improve Andreas's lot after his mother died. Andreas did not know what had happened to his father. It had never bothered him much; only lately, he had begun to wish he had more answers. He just knew that his mother had come to Castle Kragenberg alone and pregnant, seeking her brother's help. As Andreas's uncle and his mother's only living relative, Brother Stefan had arranged for Andreas to live in the castle and to take lessons with the other boys, but he could not do anything about the treatment meted out to Andreas as an orphan without any social status. Andreas had learned the value of keeping his head down. But he found it increasingly difficult to do so. Soon he would be fourteen and too old to continue taking lessons with the other pages. He sighed and then without further comment turned to help Oswald get the birds ready.

The hunting birds sat quietly on their perches, only occasionally lifting a foot or shaking out their wings, to the sound of little bells tinkling gently. All hunting birds wore these bells to help falconers find them if they went astray. Three birds were going out today, a goshawk and a lanner falcon, both fully trained and used to being handled, and a young female peregrine in training. Andreas liked the peregrine.

Oswald joked that Andreas and the peregrine were about the same age as far as their respective learning was concerned. "I don't know what you see in that bird! Maybe it's because you both have birdbrains!" he chaffed.

"I just like her. I don't know why," Andreas said. Nobody knew where the peregrine came from. Count Cuno had brought her home from one of his trips a few months ago. Rumor had it that he won her from another knight after defeating him in a joust. According to Oswald, the blue coloring of her legs and down feathers was a demerit and made her less valuable, but Andreas thought she was beautiful.

"You should see Adela when she is in full flight and the sun light catches the white feathers of her neck and belly, set off by black bars. It's magical," Andreas had told Tom one afternoon, trying to get him excited.

"Why do you call her that?" Tom, his only friend among the pages, had asked.

"Oh, you know—remember how Brother Stefan talked about Adela, the daughter of William the Conqueror, the one who acted as regent for her husband repeatedly? I think Adela is a perfect name for a proud and noble bird."

Tom had laughed. "I can never figure out how you can remember things like that from Brother Stefan's lessons!"

Now, talking gently to the young falcon to keep her calm and relaxed, Andreas checked her jesses and the little bell on her foot, and then placed her in the traveling basket.

Oswald closed the lid of the goshawk's basket and picked it up. "You carry the other two. Let's go."

By the time they reached the field near the swamp where the hunt was to be opened, the early morning mist had lifted. Andreas shivered in his thin jerkin and tunic. He could feel the damp seep into the hole in his right boot. But he forgot every sense of discomfort when he saw the huntsman lift the horn to his lips. The sunlight bounced off the polished surface of the horn as the huntsman brought forth the piercingly sweet, long, high notes announcing the opening of the hunt. *Halali! Halali!*

The hunt party consisted of Ethelbert, Count Cuno's eldest son, several neighboring landowners, squires, and knights, as well as numerous servants and attendants. Andreas's task was to keep an eye on the birds waiting for their turns and to hand needed items to Oswald from the equipment basket.

The last note trilled and faded, followed by suspenseful silence. Then a bird rose swiftly into the sky, and Ethelbert released the first falcon of the day. The hounds resumed their baying. The lanner falcon, a mere speck against the bright blue sky, wheeled in wide arcs high above the cluster of men and horses. Straining his ears, Andreas thought he could hear the tinkle of the bells on the falcon's feet. Then, in a movement too fast to follow, the falcon hurtled through the air in pursuit of a pigeon. Andreas could no longer see the pigeon, but he knew that the lanner had been successful. There had been something in that lethal self-assurance of the falcon's attack that spelled a quick death for a hapless prey.

The lanner landed on the ground and hovered over its kill.

Ethelbert watched him, a broad grin on his face.

Oswald, who stood next to him, murmured, "My lord, it is important to reward the bird." Ethelbert complied and went to the falcon, though Andreas thought he looked sulky at the reminder. The bird was well trained. Compliantly, it stepped onto Ethelbert's gloved arm and accepted his tribute.

This was the third time that Ethelbert flew falcons in a hunt. His father, Count Cuno, was an experienced falconer and wanted his son to learn the art. Harsh and with little patience with his son, Count Cuno had charged Oswald with instructing Ethelbert in falconry. Oswald was not happy about this. He knew Ethelbert too well to trust him with the valuable and volatile birds, but could not refuse a direct order to bring them. Today was going to be particularly challenging. Count Cuno was away, and there was nobody to keep Ethelbert in check.

Andreas watched Ethelbert out of the corner of his eye. The

tall, lanky boy was mean and unpredictable. However, the first half hour went by without any mishaps. The goshawk, flying fast and low to the ground, caught a partridge that the dogs had chased out the bushes. Pleased with his success, Ethelbert acquitted himself well, feeding the bird without prompting by Oswald. Now, he wanted to fly the young peregrine.

The hounds moved closer to the swamp, sniffing the ground and momentarily quiet in their intent search for prey. Peering between the men standing around, Andreas saw the gray and white feathers of a heron in the reeds.

Oswald brought Adela over to Ethelbert. "Here she is, my lord. Give her time to settle."

Ethelbert scowled. He pulled off the peregrine's hood abruptly. Without waiting for the dogs to flush out the heron, he raised his arm and pushed Adela into the air. The young falcon wobbled before she caught herself; then she flew swiftly upward before banking sharply to the left. She had her eye on another prey—a young hare in the grass near a clump of brambleberry bushes, munching clover and oblivious to its surroundings. Adela swooped down and fell on the hare. The heron lifted off, sailing away over the swamp.

Ethelbert cursed. Impatiently, he brushed past Andreas, standing close by with Adela's basket. The falcon was intent on the hare and did not move when Ethelbert reached her. He threw the carcass of the hare into the weeds and seized Adela roughly by her jesses. Before she could settle on his arm, Ethelbert tried to force the hood on her head. Frustrated and frightened, Adela struggled, scraping Ethelbert's cheek with one of her talons. Ethelbert yelped and shook her off. She landed hard on the ground and lay there as if stunned.

Andreas reacted without thinking. Afraid for Adela, he rushed forward and turned the basket directly over her like a sheltering tent.

"Well done," Oswald said quietly. He had moved with a speed that belied his years and was already next to Andreas. He reached underneath the makeshift shelter and grabbed the falcon's jesses. Andreas upended the basket. Oswald fed the agitated bird a piece of meat, gently slipped the hood over her head, and placed her into the basket. Andreas immediately closed the cover.

"That bird should be destroyed! Take it away!" Ethelbert yelled. Andreas tightened his grip on the basket. The other members of the hunt party had fallen silent. Lady Bertha, mounted on a horse large enough to accommodate her generous proportions, had an expression of polite indifference on her face; after a moment, she turned away and began to chat with another neighbor.

Oswald gaped at Ethelbert, stunned and momentarily speechless. Then he said in a placating tone, "But, my lord, it was a mistake. The peregrine did not mean to hurt you."

"I don't care. It is not fit for a lord. How dare you question me? I will tell my father about this. Take it away! I don't want to see it again!" Ethelbert's voice rose to a screech. A line of spittle ran out of the corner of his mouth, mingling with the blood from the gash on his cheek.

Oswald glanced away as if preoccupied with some hunting equipment that lay on the ground.

"Look at me when I talk to you!" Ethelbert shouted. "I expect you to obey."

Oswald faced Ethelbert, his eyes steady and calm. After a moment, he turned away and motioned to Andreas to pick up Adela's basket.

Chapter 2

"OSWALD, HE CAN'T DO THIS!"

The birds in the mews were restless. Oswald had placed Adela on her perch. He stood in front of the falcon, staring at her silently and as if unsure where to turn next.

Perplexed, Andreas watched the old man. "You are not going to do this, are you?"

"Do your chores, Andreas."

"I will, I will, but talk to me! Tell me that you are not going to kill Adela!"

Oswald turned and went to sit down on a pile of hay. He raised his head, showing Andreas a tired and defeated face. "I am only the falconer. I have to obey. I have no choice."

Andreas was stunned. "But, Oswald, you can't kill her for something that was not her fault! Hide her!"

"I can't do that. Ethelbert is probably bitterly regretting what happened, but everybody heard him. It can't be undone, and I cannot go against a direct order of my lord. If I complained to Count Cuno, he would have to take his son's side." Oswald bent his head over a piece of leather in his hands, twisting it and stretching it out again. "Don't you understand—I can't risk my family over this!" After a moment, he went on in a flat and matter-of-fact tone, "Anyway, I wouldn't even have a place to hide her. You know the law. Look, I'll give her a night. I can't face this right now anyway."

Andreas was silent. It was unbelievable that Oswald would kill Adela like a chicken about to go into the frying pan.

"But, Oswald, what if I did it? I could hide her! Nobody would ever know!"

Without responding, Oswald stood up and turned to the shelf behind him. He busied himself with sorting through some of the equipment from the morning's hunt. Andreas watched his back. Oswald moved stiffly as if his bones hurt.

Andreas opened his mouth to speak and then stopped. Instead, he got up and brushed his hands off. "I have to go to my lesson. I'll see you later."

Oswald did not turn around, just grunted in acknowledgment.

Andreas went outside and ran across the courtyard to the kitchen entrance. The smell of onions, leeks, and barley, simmering for the midmorning meal, made his stomach growl. He grabbed a piece of bread that lay on the table before the cook could snatch it away.

"Get off with you, you bread thief!" Matilda scolded, waving the rolling pin at him.

Andreas ducked as he ran past. By the time he reached the room where the sons of Count Cuno and the pages had their lessons, he had wolfed down the bread. He brushed the crumbs off his jerkin and entered.

When Andreas opened the door, Brother Stefan briefly looked around from the large wax tablet on the wall he had been writing on. He had this tablet made to his specifications. "Students have to see as well as hear in order to learn!" he told Andreas one day.

Today, Brother Stefan's clean-shaven face, with its rounded cheeks, bore its customary bland expression. He refrained from saying anything as Andreas squeezed into a seat next to his friend Tom. Tom looked intently at his slate as if concentrating on the lesson.

The room smelled of damp footgear and unwashed bodies. Andreas was unable to pay attention. While his uncle talked about Archimedes's floating bodies and filled the tablet on the wall with circles, triangles, curves, hemispheres, Andreas's thoughts drifted back to Adela, looking haughty and aloof on her perch, blissfully unaware of the doom hanging over her. Oswald had told Andreas about people having their hands cut off for being caught with a hunting bird above their station. The penalty for stealing was severe as well. He knew of a thief who had been sentenced at the manorial court and had his ear cut off before he was driven from the county. Andreas tried to picture Oswald killing Adela. He could not bear thinking about it.

At the end of the lesson, Andreas lagged behind while the other students filed out. Andreas wanted to walk his uncle back to the monastery. It always was his favorite part of the day. Brother Stefan nodded to him as he pushed his quill and several folios into his satchel. They walked out of the room and down the long, cool stone hallway.

The grandfather of the present lord had married a rich wife and used the dowry to build portions of the castle with stone rather than the customary wood. It made for a cooler building in the summer months albeit a damp and raw one in the winter unless the fires were always well stoked. Castle Kragenberg was located in the northern part of the Holy Roman Empire, just south of the city of Lübeck in the Duchy of Saxony, in a wide open, mostly flat, fertile region, and winters were harsh.

It was bright and warm in the courtyard, sheltered from the wind that blew across the fields. Andreas thought of Adela never again preening herself in the sunlight. He shook his head and followed his uncle across the courtyard.

"Your mind was not on the lesson today, was it, Andreas?" his uncle chided him gently.

"No, Uncle, I am sorry." For a moment, Andreas was tempted to tell his uncle about Adela. But he let it go; there seemed no point in burdening him with this.

Instead, while they walked on the narrow path toward the monastery, Andreas told his uncle about rescuing the merlin.

"They called you names again?"

Andreas was silent. His stomach clenched when he thought of the boys taunting him. They called him "orphan boy," "kitchen boy," and "Matilda's pet," and said awful things about his mother. "Your mother was a bit free with her favors, wasn't she? Your father was a wastrel! You don't even know where he is!"

Brother Stefan sighed. "You know that this will only get worse. They will keep picking on you until your position is clearer. Perhaps I didn't do you any favor by arranging for you to live in the castle and to take classes with Count Cuno's sons."

Glancing at his uncle from the side, Andreas thought he suddenly looked a lot older than his thirty-seven years. Andreas shook his head. "It's not so bad. I can handle it."

His uncle did not respond, just went on walking. At the monastery gate, he said, "Thank you for keeping me company." He sketched the sign of the cross. "Bless you." Then he turned to go inside, his brown cloak flapping in the wind.

The gate clanged shut. For a moment, Andreas looked at the iron panel with the tiny peephole and the high redbrick wall that enclosed the monastery; it made him feel sad and alone. Then he remembered Adela. He ran back to the castle. The field next to the path had just been freshly plowed, and he could smell the sweet, dark sod.

Chapter 3

WHEN ANDREAS TROTTED UP THE HILL TOWARD THE CASTLE, he heard a commotion near the stables. Coming around the corner, he saw men chasing the large sow. She squealed and thundered through the yard—a demented four-hundred-pound fiend. Matilda stood near the kitchen door. Her face flushed, she held a broom in her hand like a sword and yelled at the men, beside herself with rage. "How could you let that pig escape? Look at the mess she made in my kitchen!"

Maria, Oswald's granddaughter, ran up to Andreas, her braids flying. "You missed all the fun! The sow broke out of her pen. She knocked over the basin full of yeast, water, and flour set to rise. She started to eat it, when Matilda saw her and got furious. She dumped a whole big pot of hot water on her—the cleanest pig ever." Maria giggled. She grabbed Andreas's hand. "Look, they are still trying to catch her."

Andreas laughed. "Well, I guess there won't be any fresh bread for supper."

The feel of her sticky hand in his reminded him of the day when he had hidden in the stable loft after his mother died. He had been sitting in a pile of straw and crying, when a small warm body snuggled up against him. Maria had talked to him in her light voice, telling him a long, nonsensical story as if she was talking to a baby sheep. She had been hardly more than a toddler, but she had known where to find him. Eventually, they had fallen asleep in the warmth of the loft.

Andreas slung an arm around her shoulders affectionately. She still was hardly half his size. The terrified pig ran right past them, with a speed that astounded Andreas. Then it all came to an abrupt end when Matilda stuck out her broom and tripped the pig on its mad dash past the cook. Andreas and Maria watched several men subdue the squealing sow and drag her back to her pen.

Andreas said, "Well, I better go to the kitchen. I don't want to give Matilda more cause for aggravation."

Maria grinned at him. "I'm going to visit Mila's puppies; that's much more fun."

For the rest of the afternoon, Andreas helped in the kitchen. Count Cuno, upon his marriage, had constructed a separate wing for the kitchen, and it was linked to the main hall by a long stone hallway. On Lady Bertha's estate, the kitchen area was integrated into the great hall—everything smelled of smoke and cooking grease. Andreas liked the arrangement at Castle Kragenberg better.

Matilda looked disheveled. Her cap was askew, wisps of hair were plastered on her sweaty forehead, and there was a large blotch down her skirt from her encounter with the sow, but she was as fierce and demanding as ever. She made him scrub the floor and sweep up in the hallway. She gave him a pile of tallow candles and had him trim the wicks. Eventually, she handed him a basket filled with honey cakes. "Take this to the hall and place it on one of the sideboards. Also, ask the castellan whether he needs any ale."

Glad to leave the hot kitchen, Andreas walked along the stone corridor. The sideboards in the great hall had been prepared for the evening meal, and a maid had already lit some of the torches. Andreas stopped in front of the large tapestry.

During the day, the tapestry looked flat and dull. Now, bathed in the flickering light from the torches, it sprang to life. Lords and ladies, dressed in rich brocades and flowing gowns, milled about on horses at the outset of a hunt. A sumptuously dressed rider with an embroidered cap on his dark blond hair in the center held a peregrine falcon on his fist. The horses were splendidly arrayed with gilt-embossed bridles and saddle blankets hung with tassels. Even the pages and squires wore colorful clothes. Hunting dogs of various sizes looked as if they were about to take off into the forest. Toward the left, a squire blew a horn. Small birds circled above the treetops of the woods in the distance. The edge of the tapestry was filled with flowers and plants, with hares, pheasants, a robin, and even a frog, peeping out from the leaves.

Andreas gazed at the scene hungrily. It was as if Oswald's stories came to life in front of him. The rider in the center could well be one of the emperor's sons, perhaps King Manfred, known for his love of falcons; the one next to him with his shock of red hair could be his half brother King Enzio, the favorite son. The emperor called him *falconello*, the "little falcon." Sometimes Andreas pretended his father was one of the squires, perhaps the tall one in the back, or one of the knights next to the redheaded rider. Then, for a moment, it was as if the falconer standing in the front with his basket, leather hoods, extra jesses, and bells seemed to acquire his own features. Andreas studied the falcon. The weavers of the tapestry had not gotten the coloring right, but had succeeded in conveying its haughty posture. If only he could bring Adela to someone like King Enzio! A clanging noise from the kitchen recalled Andreas to his duty.

All afternoon, Andreas's thoughts circled around the problem. Maybe there might be a way to save Adela that did not involve Oswald directly. Perhaps Lady Bertha could take the falcon. No, Lady Bertha would not want to challenge the order of things any more than Oswald. Andreas decided he would go back to the mews after he finished his chores, as he often did. Usually at that time, Oswald sat peacefully in a corner, mending something or making a toy for one of his grandchildren. That would be a good time to talk to him.

The courtyard was quiet when Andreas finally left the kitchen. Some traders from the south had arrived the day before. Many of the men were probably off in the tavern, trying to find out if the traders had any news. People in the northern German regions worried about being drawn into the growing tensions between the Ghibellines, the faction supporting Emperor Frederick II, and the Guelphs, a faction that had been fighting the Hohenstaufen emperors for generations and was allied with the pope. According to Brother Stefan, Pope Gregory IX had even excommunicated the emperor and all his followers. They were not permitted to attend mass or receive the last rites, and all churches were barred to them. Andreas found this a terrifying thought. But he did not care to know more; it seemed far away and had nothing to do with his life.

When Andreas walked across the courtyard, the afternoon sunlight slanted across the western wall, transforming the normally dour gray stone facade of the castle into a glowing, warm, and sturdy structure. He slipped into the mews and called out softly, "Oswald?" There was no response; all he heard was the rustling and gentle shifting of the birds on their perches. Oswald must have gone off to the tavern. Then he noticed something unusual.

Normally, Oswald was meticulous to a fault. He kept the mews spotless and returned all equipment to its proper place in the back room when he was done with it. "A clean mews makes for healthy birds," he always said sternly.

The sight of a basket lying on its side in the corner was puzzling. It was an old basket that Oswald had mended and set aside as a backup. A set of jesses spilled out of it. An old hawking glove lay inside. Andreas bent to pick up the basket to take it to the equipment room. As he touched it, he froze, looking around in the half-light of the mews. That was it. He knew what he was going to do.

He would take Adela to his hut in the woods. Nobody would look for her there.

Chapter 4

ANDREAS HAD DISCOVERED THE ABANDONED HUT DURING ONE of his many forays into the woods. It was completely overgrown with vines. He had left the vines in place, only loosened some of them so that he could slip in and out.

Gradually, he refashioned the hut to his satisfaction. He swept the hard-packed mud floor with a straw broom and repaired the shutter over the window opening. A log served as a chair and a discarded wooden board as a table. He even had a pallet made out of an old burlap bag stuffed with straw. Next to a chipped earthenware jug and a dented wooden cup, a bowl on the table contained tallow candle stumps he had collected when helping to clean up the great hall after meals. He hung a few bunches of dried lavender flowers on a nail in the wall.

He remembered his mother's deft hands folding up scraps of linen to form little bags, filling them with the dry silvery blue flowers, and securing each with a ribbon. She placed the fragrant pouches in the linen chest, the closet, and under the blankets. At night, when she came to check on him, he used to pretend to be asleep already. He breathed in the sweet, spicy scent when she let her cool hand linger on his cheek.

People in the village were frightened of this area. The swamp gave off a pungent smell. The undergrowth along the edge was thick, with only a few gnarly oak trees sticking above the tangle of vines like deranged giants. There were rumors about somebody having taken his own life there, and people said that his restless spirit rose out of the swamp at dusk to haunt unsuspecting passersby.

Andreas had heard the villagers talk about it in whispers. "I have seen him haunt the woods with my own eyes. It's a bad place to go when the fog is rising."

"He killed someone. My grandmother told me."

"I heard that he is condemned to haunt the forest forever in punishment for taking his own life and that of another."

People who ventured too close to the swamp found themselves up to their knees in thick oozing mud, sinking further down unless someone threw out a helping hand or a rope. The swamp was said to be riddled with drowned souls; at night, their staring eyes would glimmer like stars in the soggy wasteland.

Andreas liked the solitude and stillness. The rumors and fears that kept other people away from this area in the woods did not bother him. To him, these were just stories and hardly as vivid as the stories his mother used to tell him, sitting on a stool next to his pallet at night, with her hands busy with needle and thread.

"A long, long time ago, somewhere, I cannot tell you exactly where," she always began. Her stories were populated by witches, magical firebirds, and fierce immortal ghouls in deep forests full of surprises. Often, she would take a story that he knew by heart and change it in the retelling, and they would end up laughing and laughing, trying to outdo each other by adding characters and devising alternate endings.

No, being alone in the woods did not trouble him. The hut would be a perfect sanctuary for Adela.

But, standing in the quiet mews, Andreas shivered. He envisioned himself outside the castle, with the drawbridge pulled up and the gates locked. Chances were that if he got caught, the punishment would be much worse than simply being sent on his way.

Something soft brushed past his legs. Andreas started, shocked as if he had already been caught in the act. But it was only the cat that lived in the mews. He could hear it purring. He shook his head. He could not waste any more time.

He looked around to see whether there was anything that might come in handy. He grabbed a couple of old rags and a waterskin. In another bin, Oswald had set out scraps of chicken and freshly killed mice for the next day's feeding. Andreas found an iron hook in a pile of tools set aside for straightening by the blacksmith. Bent and rusty as it was, it was going to be adequate to the task.

Adela sat on the perch closest to the wall. She was weaving

back and forth on her perch. Andreas had seen horses do this when they were bored or restless. Perhaps she was still confused by the day's events and the experience of being thrown onto the ground.

Andreas could hear himself breathing. He needed to act before it got completely dark and while there was nobody around.

Andreas put everything he needed into a satchel and hung it over his shoulder. He slipped the hood over Adela's head while talking to her in a low tone. "Adela, you are going to be safe. I have a good place for you. I will take care of you. Don't worry." She was used to the sound of his voice and willingly shifted to his arm and from there into the traveling basket. Before he left the mews, he peered outside. The sun had gone down, and the courtyard was quiet.

Quickly, he made his way to the little gate on the back wall. The gate was rarely locked. The builder of the original castle, Count Cuno's grandfather, had set the castle on a hill. The moat extended only around the front half of the building complex; in the back, the only protection was a high stone wall that bordered on a dense forest on the slope. Beyond the gate, a series of steep stone steps led into an orchard.

The old apple trees were covered in blossoms, in the halflight of the dusk looking like bowlegged old women with frizzy silvery hair. They would shelter him against anyone looking out of the castle on that side. He reached the stone wall on the edge of the orchard. The outer gate made a creaking noise when he opened it. He bit his lip and waited anxiously, but there were no sounds of alarm from the castle compound. He passed through, gently pulling it closed behind him. The forest came up to the stone wall, and underneath the dense canopy of oaks and pines Andreas felt safe from prying eyes.

It was dark when he got to the hut. With a few twigs and his striker kit—a flint stone and a piece of iron—he made small fire and lit several of his precious tallow candle stumps before the flames died down. Then he set up a makeshift perch for Adela. He used an old tree trunk, with a smooth surface, which Andreas had thought of turning into a chair. He attached the hook to it, so that he could secure the jesses. Finally, he opened the basket. Adela willingly stepped onto his arm and from there on to the perch.

Andreas studied her. The weaving movement from earlier had stopped. She looked content.

"Adela, I have to get back. I will be back tomorrow to check on you. Don't worry." Andreas blew out the candles and pulled the door shut behind him.

When Andreas reached the castle wall, his face and back dripped in sweat. He listened for sounds from the courtyard, but it was quiet. Quickly, he slipped through the gate. Two dogs ran up to him, snuffling and wagging their tails. He walked over to the well, pulled up a bucket of water, and dumped it over his head, wiping his hands and face.

Then he went to the dormitory, located in a semi-detached part of the main building. By the time he reached the dark room that he shared with Thomas and two other boys, he trembled from exhaustion and the release of tension. Fortunately, the others were fast asleep. He did not think he could have dealt with any questions. He pulled off his wet tunic and sat down on his pallet. He rubbed his ear. Getting it cut off had to hurt. He winced at the thought. No, this would not happen. He would not let them catch him.

PART II

UNCERTAIN SANCTUARY

On Calling a Peregrine to the Lure

"It is necessary for falcons trained to hawk at the brook to ring up and wait on above the falconer, in order to capture those birds sent up for her. The more directly the peregrine soars above the falconer who is putting up the quarry, the more easily she descends upon the prey, irrespective of the direction in which it is served. It is chiefly through her love of the lure itself that a peregrine is taught to wait on right over the falconer; and the greater her liking for that decoy, the more prompt will be her response to her master's call."

- Frederick of Hohenstaufen, *The Art of Falconry: Being the De Arte Venandi Cum Avibus of Frederick II of Hohenstaufen*

Chapter 5

"COME ON, ANDREAS! GET UP! IT'S LATE!" TOM WAS SHAKING him. "Where were you last night?"

Andreas groaned, trying to wake up. He rubbed his eyes and opened his mouth. Then, looking up at Tom's concerned face, he stopped himself. Somebody might overhear. Besides, he did not want to put Tom in an awkward position. He yawned to cover the silence.

Together they ran down to the kitchen and from there to their respective chores. Andreas slowed down as he approached the mews. He had no idea what to say to Oswald.

When Andreas walked into the mews, he saw Oswald furiously scrubbing the cobblestones at the entrance.

"A fox got into the mews last night. I forgot to latch the gate in the back, and he must have pushed his way inside. He got the peregrine. Help me clean up." Oswald spoke brusquely, without stopping what he was doing.

"A fox?" Peering over Oswald's shoulder, Andres saw a dark stain in the middle of the aisle. A bag of grain had burst open and spilled along the wall. He tried to get a closer look at the stain, but found Oswald blocking his way.

"Do I have to repeat myself? Get moving! You know where the broom is!"

"Oswald, I..." Andreas began hesitantly, although in truth still unsure of what to say.

Oswald cut in before Andreas could continue. "What are you waiting for? We have a lot to do today."

Oswald had never spoken so sharply to him. Momentarily stung, Andreas went into the equipment room and fetched a broom.

They worked silently, cleaning the mews, feeding the birds,

and straightening out the equipment. Oswald continued to be preemptory and harsh, refusing to engage in any conversation whatsoever. They were done much sooner than usual.

"Go on, get out of here. I need some peace and quiet," Oswald said gruffly.

In the courtyard, stable boys were brushing horses. A field hand sat near the barn, surrounded by tools, and was scraping rust off a plow. Andreas could hear the usual noises from the kitchen— scolding by Matilda, the servants' laughter, and pots banging. He had just enough time to go to the woods and check on Adela.

By the time Andreas got to the hut, the sun was almost directly overhead. Adela flapped her wings almost as if she had been waiting for him. He cleaned up around her perch and filled her water bowl, although he knew that like other birds of prey Adela got most of her water from her food. He fed Adela with the meat he had scavenged from the bin in the mews; from now on, he had to make sure to come early in the morning. Hunting birds should not be fed at midday.

Andreas did not dare to fly her, but he thought she could use some fresh air. He grabbed the old hawking gloves that he had taken along the night before. Gingerly, Adela stepped onto his arm. After securing her hood, he walked outside and down the wood trail until he got to the little glade. Gently, he slipped the hood off her head. For a moment, he caught a full view of the dark spots underneath her eyes; they made her look pugnacious and ready to fend off attackers. Oswald had explained to him that these spots helped to deflect the glare from the sunlight.

Adela made a few hopping movements and then settled down on his arm. Andreas walked around the perimeter of the glade, letting her take everything in and get used to her surroundings. It was peaceful in the woods. Reluctantly, he headed back to the hut. He would be missed if he did not return soon.

In the mews, he tried to talk to Oswald and found himself cut off immediately. "I don't have time to stand here and jaw endlessly. There is work to be done."

Confounded and yet secretly relieved, Andreas bent to his work.

A day after Adela had taken up residence in the hut, Oswald barked at Andreas to get rid of some rubbish piled up in a dark corner in the mews. When Andreas poked at the rubbish with a shovel, he found a clump of leather stitched into the shape of a tiny bird. It was an old lure. Falconers trained and exercised birds by swinging lures in large circles. Looking around, Andreas saw Oswald's back turned to him and quickly grabbed it. Pleased with his find, he ventured into the equipment room when Oswald had left the mews and found a string that looked worn but strong and long enough. Now he had everything he needed.

Over the next few weeks, Andreas got up before first light every morning and ran to the hut. Adela eagerly stepped on his arm when it came time for her outing. Finally, Andreas decided it was time to fly her. He used the lure as Oswald had taught him. Wheeling it about, he was careful to keep the circles low, afraid that he would not be able to recall the young falcon if she went much beyond tree level. But it was as if they had worked together for months. Andreas grinned with delight as he watched the falcon swoop around him. Then he brought her back to the fist and fed her a little reward. He gradually increased the size of the circles, and had her make more passes at the lure before letting her claim her reward. By now, she easily and willingly returned to his glove and responded to his call.

One morning, he flew her properly. He did not feed her before he took her out; thus she would have an incentive to return when he called her. He walked with her to a clearing in the woods. He waited until he could see some birds in the vicinity and then launched her into the air. She began to circle the area. With bated breath, Andreas squinted up at the falcon. Suddenly, in the blink of an eye, she folded her wings and started her stoop. She hurtled toward the ground so rapidly that Andreas was not even able to make out her target before she was upon it. She had caught a quail that emerged out of the bushes on the side of the clearing.

To his immense gratification, Adela willingly returned to his glove when he called. She accepted the piece of meat he held out to her and then sat quietly on his arm, glancing around with her shiny black eyes, alert but steady.

"You caught your own food today! You flew beautifully," Andreas said proudly as he slipped the hood over her head, before taking her back to the hut.

That morning, even though he had run most of the way, he still was late by the time he got back to the castle, and class had already started. Several boys looked up when he slid into the room. Andreas avoided meeting their eyes and sat down next to Tom. Tom was doodling on his wax tablet; he gave Andreas a quick nod and a smile.

Brother Stefan sat at his desk, an open manuscript in front of him, and was reading to the class. He looked up. "Andreas, thank you for joining us. Would you kindly share with us your understanding of the role of the chorus in the comedies of Aristophanes?"

Andreas heard a muffled snigger behind him. He quickly stood up, crimson with embarrassment. "The role of the chorus . . ." he started in a low voice. Then, as he spoke, he forgot his embarrassment and concluded firmly, "Aristophanes used the chorus as a mirror—to reflect the voice of the people and his own commentary." He enjoyed his uncle's description of the plays and their political undertones.

As it often happened, Andreas had forgotten that his ability to answer was unlikely to endear himself to the others. When he sat down, he caught a smirk on Ethelbert's face. Andreas glanced away, pretending to be absorbed in the contents of his satchel.

Meanwhile, Brother Stefan had moved on to Latin. He called on Tom to decline the verb *currere* "to run." Tom got up and after a brief hesitation declaimed, "*Curro, curris, currit...* I run, you run, he runs . . ." and so the lesson continued.

After class, Andreas waited in the hallway for Tom to join him. Ethelbert swiftly kicked Andreas in the shin as he squeezed past the boy. The wound on Ethelbert's cheek had turned into a dark, scabbed line. Andreas did not have time to react because Dietl and Tilman, two of the older pages, challenged him.

"So, what are you doing at night these days? Found a soft pillow somewhere, did you? I never thought that our kitchen boy had it in him!" Leering suggestively, they shoved their faces directly into

Andreas's line of sight. "How about taking us along next time? We could show you some tricks!"

Andreas, with his leg smarting from the kick, stayed leaning against the wall and tried to keep his expression blank.

They pulled on his tunic. "Come; let us help fix you up! This outfit won't win you any favors!"

Andreas kept his curled fists out of sight while eyeing the boys to determine whom he should charge first, when Tom peered around the corner.

Tom frowned and walked back toward the boys. "This is a fine way for future squires to behave. Don't you know better than that? Anyway, I heard the castellan walking down the hallway!" There was a note of authority in his voice, despite his general air of friendly affability and good humor. The boys scattered, while Tom and Andreas went out together.

"You have to stop protecting me! I can handle this," Andreas said.

"Oh, come on, you know that it is pointless to let them provoke

you into a fight. All it does is to get you in trouble. You used to be smarter about this. You need to buy some time until you know what you are going to do."

Andreas shook his head in frustration. "But that's the whole point. How can I figure out what I am going to do, when I cannot make a single move in any direction without acting above my station or alienating people because Brother Stefan taught me Latin? So what difference does it make if I get in trouble now and then? At least, I would get some satisfaction!"

Tom did not respond to this, just slung his arm over Andreas's shoulders affectionately. Acting upon unspoken consent, the two friends went out of the courtyard to the bridge across the moat. On the other side of the moat, they sat down at the foot of an ancient willow tree. The roots bulged out, creating little hollows and caves. Andreas and Tom had used these spaces for hiding treasures when they were younger. Idly, Andreas tossed bits of wood and tiny pebbles into the moat.

"So what's going on? Come on, tell Uncle Tom all about it!"

Andreas looked at Tom's open friendly face adorned with freckles and once again, as so many times before, thought of his own dark hair and accentuated cheekbones with a pang. He was tired of being different. He frowned, trying to figure out what to say. He did not want to talk about Adela. It was too dangerous a secret.

"I had another run in with Gerd and his buddies," Andreas said finally. He told Tom about finding the merlin and chasing off the village boys. "I want to stuff Gerd into the duck pond—and Ethelbert right along."

"I don't blame you, but what good would that do? Besides, if the castellan hears of you getting into a fight, you'll get whipped," Tom said reasonably.

"Yes, you're right. Still, it might almost be worth it."

Tom was the son of a squire and served as a page; the boys from the village would be careful before challenging him. Andreas sometimes helped Tom with his letters and his math and geometry exercises. Tom was shorter than most of his age-mates and tended toward the chubby. He often got teased for this, but he laughed along with his tormentors, which completely disarmed them.

Tom chuckled. "I can't say that I blame you. I am beginning to find Ethelbert truly irksome. He thinks he can lord it above everybody else just because he is the son of Count Cuno. This is not going to be a good place when he takes over. When I have become a knight, I can't wait to join King Conrad in Bavaria. I wish you could come with me." The boys had gone over this many times, trying to find a place for Andreas in this scheme.

Andreas rubbed the coarse fabric of his tunic between his fingers. "Sometimes I envy you. You know exactly what you are going to be. And you have your family. There is no place for me to go to."

"Come on, Andreas. What is this, your day for feeling sorry for yourself? You have your uncle. More importantly you have your brains—that's a lot more than many people have."

For a moment, Tom's abrasiveness grated. Then Andreas nodded. "You are right. Anyway, I will figure something out. Maybe I will become a mercenary!" He spoke flippantly to cover his anxiety.

"So what have you been doing to make you fall asleep in class?" Tom inquired casually.

Andreas glanced at him sideways. "Tom, what if I told you that it is better for you not to know?"

"Ah, well, I have a pretty good idea. I notice things even if you think I never pay attention. Don't worry. I won't ask again." Tom picked up a stick and started peeling away the bark, looking intently at his hands while he talked. "But I think that this is not a good place for you anymore. You are much smarter than I about bookish things, but you are clueless when it comes to the real world. You will keep running up against all the Ethelberts of this world. You chafe against the rules that restrict everyone, even those with land or title or a trade."

Andreas was taken aback by the blunt words. He started to defend himself, "I know I can't get around the rules. You sound like Brother Stefan. Besides, don't we all bend the rules sometimes?"

Tom said, "Well, there are degrees of bending. But you are just asking for trouble every day, and you will end up getting badly hurt. You need to figure out what you want to do, and I don't think it can be here. There is nothing here for you."

"You are here," Andreas said, dismayed by Tom's description.

"True for now, but I will leave soon to assume my position as a squire at the court of King Conrad. And once I am knighted—well, since my father has no land to leave me, I might eventually go east and join the Teutonic knights to help settle the Prussians. What about that?"

Andreas looked at him with affection. "This is the first time you have talked about this. This is a grand idea. It makes me think that becoming a mercenary might not be such a bad thing; at least it would get me out of here!"

"Well, something tells me that you'd be hopeless as a mercenary—constantly worrying about the horses being off their feed or picking up orphaned rabbits on the road; still, it would be better than what you are doing now—which is just dreaming, drifting, and waiting for trouble." Tom tossed the stick into the water. Then he cuffed Andreas in the side. "I can just see it— you'll end up going on a Crusade and come back, unwashed, ridden with lice, and with a beard all the way down to your belly, intoning psalms without stopping."

Andreas cuffed him back, and they started to wrestle, until Tom slipped off the edge of the bank and both boys rolled into the moat, laughing hysterically.

Chapter 6

TAKING CARE OF ADELA HAD BECOME ROUTINE. MAKING DO with less sleep, Andreas got up before first light, snitched some feed from the mews, ran to the hut, and took Adela out. The falcon had relaxed with him and responded to his cues. He was so pleased with his success that he forgot to worry about the future.

One of Count Cuno's retainers noticed Andreas when he slipped through the little gate into the castle grounds early in the morning.

"Hey, boy, what are you sneaking around for?" The burly middle-aged man grabbed Andreas by the tunic and glared at him, showing his yellowed teeth.

Trying to evade the stench of his breath, Andreas mumbled something about looking for herbs for Matilda and made his escape. After that, Andreas made a point of waiting until nobody was in sight when he came into the courtyard. On his way to the hut, he frequently checked to make sure nobody followed him.

One morning, when Andreas came back from the woods, there was an odd contraption in the middle of the courtyard, a two-wheeled cart with a flat roof and two draft animals standing in front. Andreas blinked and looked again—they seemed to be some sort of strange horse breed with very large ears and sturdy bodies. The sides of the cart were painted in bright blue and red, setting off the cheerful yellow frames around the little windows on each side. Wide bands of iron reinforced the rims and spokes of the wheels.

Oswald stood in front of the mews chatting with a stranger. The man was just a bit taller than Andreas, but solidly built. His dark hair and dark beard were neatly trimmed in odd contrast to his scruffy-looking tunic and leggings. He appeared relaxed and yet at the same time watchful.

"So, Oswald, what is that horrific structure just beyond the moat? It looks like an architect's undigested nightmare."

Oswald chuckled. "What, you don't like it? Count Cuno had the grand idea of building a rose bower with a gazebo for his wife. Only she died before the first rose could be planted. And now, it just stands there."

Andreas grinned; he and Tom used to joke about it, though secretly proud of living at the only castle in the region with such an odd and eccentric structure.

"How is trade these days, Richard? Are you transporting any gyrfalcons to Italy?"

The trader jovially clapped Oswald on the shoulders, and together they walked off toward the main entrance. "I got one that I picked up in Antwerp; he is a real beauty. Other than that, I have a lanner and a saker falcon and a merlin. To be honest, I think I am going to explore other lines of business..." Their voices grew faint. Andreas turned back to the cart.

A young woman jumped out of the back. She was plump and short, with a head of dark curly hair that strayed out from under a white kerchief. She held a blanket in her arms and began to shake it vigorously. Her cheeks were flushed, and she looked disgruntled. An older man, stocky and with a pasty, unhealthy complexion, now emerged from the cart. Without looking at her or Andreas, he went to the front of the cart and busied himself with the draft animals. One of them laid its ears back and tried to bite him. He slapped its rump, and then, without finishing what he was doing, walked off.

Andreas came closer and peered into the cart. A curtain blocked off the area closest to the front. Near the opening, across from a few boxes, containers with feed, piles of blankets, and equipment hanging from the wall, he saw five perches with birds secured on top of four of them. The bird closest to the opening clearly was the gyrfalcon the trader had talked about. Andreas had never seen one before and looked at it with fascination. It looked huge—broader-winged and longer-tailed than any hunting bird he had seen. It was nearly completely white, with only a touch of cream streaking the nape and crown, and dark spots on the wings and sides. The powerful talons stood out starkly against the yellow feet and legs; the same intense yellow outlining the eyes and beak gave it an almost malevolent look.

The falcon shook out its wings and screeched loudly. Startled, Andreas backed up and bumped into the young woman.

"Watch what you are doing!" she yelled at him.

"Oh, sorry! I heard about the gyrfalcon. I wanted to see it!" Andreas said quickly, trying to placate her.

"Oh no, another falcon lover! Well, don't you have any work to do?"

Andreas shrugged, about to walk off, when he saw an odd carving nailed to the inside of the cart's door. It looked like a man and a woman with a child in the middle; it was about as tall as two hand widths and painted in all the colors of the rainbow. He ran his hand over it. "What is that?"

"That?" The young woman glanced at him. She had finished shaking the blanket and was folding it up. "My father brought that back from Sicily. It is a wheel brake."

Andreas frowned and looked at her questioningly.

"See where the wheel would go?" The young woman pointed to the groove on the bottom of the carving. "Sicilian carts have these brakes. My father says it is a picture of Mary, Joseph, and the Christ Child. He got it as a blessing of our house—or I guess our cart!"

She grabbed a big pile of clothes from the edge of the cart. "I have to go. I have to wash these." She looked around uncertainly.

"Wait. I can show you where you need to go," Andreas said impulsively.

"You think I would not be able to find it?" She laughed at him. "All right, so show me!" Together they walked toward the stream where other women were doing their wash.

"I have never seen cart horses like yours," Andreas said.

"Paris and Helen, you mean? Those aren't horses. They are mules—much better for long journeys and pulling carts."

Andreas started to laugh. "Paris and Helen, as in the *Iliad*?

Which one is Helen?"

"Oh, can't you guess? The one that tried to bite Witold— serve him right, too. Isn't she well named? She is so perfectly evil-minded, I just adore her."

"And Paris?"

"Well, you know—typical male—half asleep most of the time. Can't you just see him as the young lover whose stupidity brought down the walls of Troy?" Laughing, the young woman bent down and began to soak some of the wash.

"How do you know about the Battle of Troy?" Andreas asked.

He knew how rare it was for girls to get an education.

"I never learned to read well, if that is what you are wondering." The girl was matter of fact in her response. "But if you spent some time around my father, you, too, would know the Greek myths like the back of your hand. He is a great storyteller."

Reluctantly, Andreas recollected his chores. "What is your name? Mine is Andreas."

"Gemma." She smiled at him. "We will be here for a few days. Come and visit. When Father goes off, I have no one to talk to but Witold, and he is getting a bit annoying to put it mildly—he can't keep his hands to himself."

During the preparation for the midday meal, Andreas walked to the great hall with a basket full of trenchers—flat pieces of stale bread used as plates.

When he came around the corner, he saw Count Cuno talking to Ethelbert in a doorway. Andreas heard snatches of the conversation: "...reckless impetuousness... haven't you learned anything... expensive hunting bird... act in accordance with your status..."

Ethelbert looked flushed and miserable. Andreas quietly stepped back. But it was too late. Ethelbert stared directly at him, his face a mix of sullen embarrassment and rage at having someone witness his humiliation. Shaken, Andreas returned to the kitchen. Ethelbert would pounce on the first opportunity to revenge himself.

Matilda raised her eyebrows when she saw Andreas. He looked at the floor as if he had dropped some of the trenchers.

Matilda shrugged and turned to the hearth, too busy to concern herself with this.

Chapter 7

DINNER IN THE HALL THAT DAY WAS A BUSY AFFAIR. COUNT Cuno had invited some of his neighbors, and the trader had also been asked to join the table. The castellan had been instructed to offer red wine in addition to the customary ale. It was Andreas's turn to help serve. The first course was a thick soup with vegetables. This was followed by smoked trout, a special delicacy. Matilda had decorated each fish with the yellow of a boiled egg to indicate the eye and the white for some of the scales and arranged them on a large platter, surrounded by parsley leaves.

Matilda grabbed Andreas before he went back to the hall with the third course. She brushed off his tunic with a few brusque movements and patted down his hair with some water from the bucket. Then she handed him a heavy terrine. He had to hold it with both hands and struggled to keep the ladle from slipping into the bowl. Andreas inhaled the aroma of the heavy spices mixed with a sauce of honey and almonds used to thicken the duck stew.

At the head of the table, Count Cuno sat next to his cousin Lady Bertha. Andreas always marveled at her ability to sit at the table and eat. She was so stout that she had to reach across her immense belly to reach the food. It did not lessen her appetite. Nonetheless, she sat a horse well and loved to hunt. Count Cuno was just toasting Lady Bertha, when a few words further down the table caught his attention.

Count Cuno knocked his spoon against his beaker and called out, "Master Richard of Brugge, what news do you bring us from Lübeck and Antwerp?" He served himself from the terrine, barely glancing at Andreas.

The dark-haired man stood up and bowed to Count Cuno. "My lord count, it is an honor to share the board with you. Indeed, I have some news to share." He sat down again and took a sip from his beaker. "Just before I left Lübeck, a courier had come up from the north of Italy." He looked around and then continued. "There was a big battle between the Lombard League and the imperial army at Fossalta on May twenty-sixth. The imperial army was defeated. King Enzio was captured alive and is now being held prisoner in Bologna."

There was a moment of silence. The other guests waited for a signal from their host to resume talking.

Count Cuno, who according to Brother Stefan had occasionally sided against the Hohenstaufen emperors, would hardly be grieved by the capture of Emperor Frederick II's favorite son. He rubbed his nose. "Thank you, Master Richard. Sometimes we are a bit isolated in our rural backwaters." He picked up a bowl and passed it down to the falcon trader. "Here, you might like some of these stewed pears with raisins and ginger. I hope you will enjoy your stay with us." Then he took a pinch of salt from the heavy silver saltcellar at his right hand and started to talk in a low voice to the knight next to him.

Andreas, walking past the diners to go back to the kitchen for another platter, noticed that Lady Bertha had dropped a lacy handkerchief onto the floor. He picked it up and tried to hand it to her.

She looked at him sharply and then smiled. "Ah, Andreas, Oswald spoke highly of you the other day."

Andreas was surprised that she knew his name. Lady Bertha waved away the handkerchief he held out. "Keep it, young man." She chuckled so that her double chin wobbled. "You never know — there might be a young lady who would be pleased to receive such a gift."

By the time the servants began to carry around cheese platters and flagons of hippocras, a wine flavored with spices, the hall was smoky and the diners were talking loudly to make themselves heard. Near the fireplace a minstrel picked out songs on his lute in a dispirited fashion; nobody paid attention to him. The tables were littered with soiled pewter bowls, fish bones, and soaked trenchers.

Dogs milled about, waiting for their chance to get at food dropped from the table.

"How are the roads these days, Master Richard?" Alhard, one

of Count Cuno's older retainers, sat next to the trader. Alhard looked wistful. "I remember that travel was not easy during the Crusade in 1228. We were plodding through mud half of the time."

"Well, yes, mud, marauders, and mayhem. Travel certainly is not for the faint of heart." Richard smiled at him. "Sometimes we end up on a Roman road—that's sheer bliss. But the other roads are not so bad. If you have a horse that's well shod or a sturdy cart, you can manage. Of course, marauders should not be taken lightly; however, some precautions such as bearing arms and traveling in groups can prevent most of the trouble. Besides, there seem to be more inns every year—if you don't mind bedbugs too much."

Alhard chuckled at his description, evidently remembering the bedbugs in his time. Another man leaned forward. "Tell us, have you been at the court of Emperor Frederick? Is it true that he collects all sorts of exotic animals?"

Richard smiled readily. "You are quite right. I have seen some of them myself. He brought many animals from the Holy Lands such as camels, leopards, and apes. And of course, it is well known that he is very knowledgeable about birds of prey. Perhaps you have heard that he is working on a book about falconry."

Alhard looked amazed. "Really? How fascinating. Where are you bound for now? I heard that you are transporting a gyrfalcon."

Richard glanced at him courteously. "Indeed I am. It is a noble bird, and it is already spoken for. Anyway, we are headed south in a few days." He did not elaborate, but the gyrfalcon could be intended only for the highest in the land; and in the south, that meant the emperor.

Andreas stood still. He held a platter full of *Krapfen*, a warm fried pastry. One slid onto the floor, to be immediately snatched up by a dog. Andreas no longer heard any of the talk around him; all the faces seemed to have vanished in the smoky haze. Only the trader's dark face remained visible. Andreas watched him pick up a piece of bread from the table and dunk it in his wine, while he chatted with his neighbors.

That's my chance, Andreas thought. He was elated and terrified at the same time. He would take Adela to the court of Emperor Frederick II.

A servant jostled Andreas and said, "Hey, Andreas, move!"

That night, Andreas could not sleep. He thought about how he could manage to hide himself in the trader's cart and how he could convince the trader to take him along, once he was discovered. When he finally fell asleep, he dreamed of leopards. Emperor Frederick II, in a gown of gold brocade and with a flowing mane of red hair, a gyrfalcon perched on his shoulder, sat on the rim of a fountain and held out his hand to three leopards. Their teeth were bared as if they were grinning, and they all looked like Ethelbert.

Chapter 8

THE NEXT MORNING, ANDREAS WAS UP EVEN EARLIER THAN usual. In the mews, before helping himself to some feed from the bin, he looked around to see whether there was anything lying about that might come in handy. He studied a pile of rags. Then he had an idea. With a few thin pieces of wood, he could construct a framework for a little tent; Adela could sit underneath, safe on a perch in the corner of the cart and able to breathe, while the rags would deflect attention, blending into the back wall of the cart. He would hide himself under a pile of rags on the floor.

When he arrived at the hut, Adela fluttered her wings excitedly, clearly anticipating her outing. She had lost all her skittishness, and her eyes looked shiny and her feathers soft and fluffy. As he carried her around and flew her to the lure, he talked to her. "Adela, we are going to the emperor. He will take you in and award you to one of his earls or lords. You will have a good life. Maybe Emperor Frederick himself will take you hunting." Oswald had told him that at Emperor Frederick II's court, pages could become valets and then falconers; some even advanced to higher office. The emperor might make him a falconer. Anyway, once he was there and the falcon safe, somehow it would all work out.

When he got back to the castle, he first went to visit Gemma and to get another look at the cart.

Gemma sat on the ground, mending some clothing. She smiled at him. "Oh, it's you. Do you want to look at the falcon again?"

"Sure." Given such an opening, Andreas peered into the interior of the cart. "May I go in for a moment?"

"Go ahead. We are not going anywhere," Gemma said, her attention back on her work. Andreas hopped inside. The cart was propped up at the front end by a wooden block, so that the two wheels and the wooden block kept it straight. It shifted only slightly under his weight. He had to bend his head, but aside from that could move around comfortably. He studied the space carefully, especially the position of the extra perch in the back. Then he hopped out again and squatted next to the young woman.

"Do you sleep in the cart?" Andreas asked.

"Not if we can help it. It gets cramped in there. Usually, we stay in an inn."

"When are you leaving?"

"Tomorrow morning. Father wants to get an early start." Gemma looked wistful. "I would not mind staying a bit longer—I like sleeping on a proper straw pallet on a clean floor. Compared to most inns that we stay at, this is heavenly. But he is anxious about getting on the road."

"Is it hard—having to travel all the time?"

Gemma smiled, shaking off her mood. "If I lived in one place, I would have to listen to someone like your Matilda, browbeating me and telling me what to do. No, the road suits me fine."

Andreas got up. "I have to go do my chores." In the kitchen, he tried to work as hard as he could. Watching him scrubbing the stone floor, Matilda looked at him oddly but did not say anything.

Then Andreas went to the classroom. He thought that he would attract less attention by following all the regular routines. Also he wanted to do this—it was like taking leave from everything that he had ever known.

The classroom was stuffy; it was the first really hot day that summer. The other boys seemed to be lost in a stupor, lethargically scratching on their tablets, while Brother Stefan read to them from Caesar's *Gallic Wars*. He drew a rough map of Europe on the wall tablet and pointed out the route the Romans took to cross the Alps. Andreas's thoughts drifted off.

"Uncle, may I talk to you?" Andreas asked as they walked out after class.

"I have some time before sext." Sext was the third prayer service of the Book of Hours and recited at noon. "I was going to work on copying the manuscript I have shown you. But I can take a break." Together they headed for the path along the field to the monastery. They walked in silence. For Brother Stefan as a

Benedictine, silence was habitual, while Andreas was unsure how to begin.

When they arrived at the gate, his uncle said, "Let's go to the garden; I want to see how much work I need to do there in the next few days."

They entered the arcade in the center of the building complex, which framed a large, rectangular sheltered garden. A few monks strolled in the arcade around a grassy area with a stone fountain in the center. Andreas and his uncle walked down its entire length, through a gate, and into another secluded smaller garden, where raised beds were filled with comfrey, lavender, sage, rosemary, madder, rue, and many other herbs. Brother Stefan led Andreas to a small wooden bench.

Fruit had begun to set on the espaliered pear trees, carefully trained against the south-facing wall. Andreas bent down and pinched a few mint leaves, momentarily soothed by the scent of the rich soil, warmed by the sun and steamy with last night's rain.

"Uncle, if I were to leave here, what would you say? Would you give me your blessing?"

Brother Stefan looked at him, his round face calm and unsurprised. "Andreas, of course, I give you my blessing. Do you want to tell me what is on your mind?"

Andreas crushed the mint leaves with his fingers. "I know that I need to do something. I can't stay doing chores for Matilda forever."

"Sometimes I have wondered how you remained so quiet and patient, whenever you got kicked or abused by the others. You just went about your way."

"It's getting harder to be patient. I can't do it anymore." Andreas studied the herbs in front of him intently.

"Come with me to my cell." His uncle got up and led the way down the cool stone hallway past several little doors until he got to his own cell. It was cool inside. There was a pallet, a wooden cross on the wall, a wooden chest, and a table with a chair underneath the narrow window set high on the wall so that looking out was not possible. His uncle sat on the chair. Andreas crouched on the floor. He had rarely spent time inside his uncle's cell.

Andreas ran his hand back and forth on the cool stone floor. He had so many questions. Most of all, it bothered him that he did not know what had happened to his father. He was silent. Finally, he asked, "Why did you become a monk?"

"Joining the order was like coming home. I found what I wanted to do. It's something that I can do well—teaching and working on manuscripts. I hope that one day you find your place in this world. I did, and there is no greater happiness than that." After a moment, he said, "But that's not really what you are asking, is it?"

Andreas blurted out, "Do you know anything about my father?

My mother never told me—I guess I was too young."

"I don't have any answers for you. All I know is that your mother loved him with all her heart."

Andreas shook his head, his eyes on the stone flags. "I just wish I knew what happened."

Andreas's eyes burned. He felt his uncle's warm hands on his head, tracing the sign of the cross. He sat silently for a few moments, his head bent. Then he said, "I have to go."

When Andreas returned to the castle, he saw Maria running with other children in the meadow on the other side of the moat. Andreas watched her for a while, and then he turned away, wistful and reassured. Maria was going to be fine.

Early that evening, Andreas went into the dormitory before anyone else was there. He had already gathered up the few personal belongings he had. He had thought that he would talk to Tom, but then had found that he could not do it. He had decided to leave a note for Tom on his writing tablet.

Andreas opened Tom's satchel and pulled out the tablet and stylus. Then he bit his lip. He had to write something that would not make trouble for Tom if someone saw it. Slowly, he scratched his message onto the wax surface of the tablet. "Don't worry about me. I promise I won't grow a beard down to my belly. Andreas." Carefully, he slid the tablet back into the satchel, together with one of Adela's fluffy white feathers from her belly stuck into the frame. Before he closed the satchel, he took a wooden knife handle from underneath his pallet. He had whittled away at the handle in secret and carved the letter *T* onto it. It was bad luck to give a knife as a present, but he hoped Tom would like the handle. He returned the satchel to its place near Tom's pallet and took another look around the cramped and stuffy dormitory. He was not going to miss this, only his latenight conversations with Tom, when everyone else was asleep.

In the mews, it was quiet; the birds did not stir when he walked in. Oswald sat in his usual corner, patiently rubbing a wood plane back and forth on a little dollhouse table he was making for Maria. He glanced up, nodded, and then bent his attention back on his work.

Andreas sat down next to him. There was nothing he could say. He looked at Oswald's swollen knobby hands with the red knuckle joints; it was as if he could feel the aching in his own bones. He wondered whether Matilda might have a salve to soothe them.

Oswald coughed. "It is strange—I never thought I would say this, but I am actually glad that Count Cuno has proposed bringing in a younger man to take over the mews. He said it is time that I lightened the burden. I can stay here with my family and work a little less." Oswald talked as if there had never been any interruption between them.

"I cannot imagine the mews without you," Andreas said. "It is a change, that's for sure," Oswald said comfortably. Andreas swallowed. "Oswald, I want to leave, too."

Oswald shook his head, suddenly appearing tense and irritated. "Of course, you can't stay here forever. But I don't want to talk about this tonight." He waved his hands impatiently. Then he looked at Andreas sternly. "We have not gone over any of the lessons in falconry lately. Let's see if you still remember anything. Tell me the most important word you need to keep in mind."

Andreas grinned at him. This was familiar territory. "Respect." "Go on."

"Four forms of respect—respect for the animal and the fact that it is not a human being; respect for the fact falcons are and should always be treated as wild animals rather than domesticated animals; respect for the natural order and the ranks of all beings, including falcons and their owners; and respect for venery as a noble art and craft of hunting with birds of prey."

Suddenly, Andreas remembered a story Oswald had told him about the emperor. There had been a saker falcon that the emperor loved. During a hunt, this falcon had abandoned the heron he was supposed to attack and turned instead on a young eagle flying in the vicinity. The falcon was separated from the eagle, and the emperor decreed that the falcon be executed on the spot by having his head cut off. In response to the stunned surprise of the people near him, the emperor supposedly said: 'The falcon killed his lord. For this, he must die.' Andreas shifted uncomfortably. He could not imagine that this had really happened. The emperor loved falcons too much; he would not do this when he met Adela.

"That will do; the rest is just chicken feed," Oswald grunted, carefully smoothing the wooden legs of the table with a wood file. "If you steer by these, you can't go wrong."

"Look, Oswald, I have something for Maria. Would you give it to her? I don't want to carry it around until it gets dirty. Lady Bertha gave it to me." Andreas burrowed under his waistband and pulled out a little lacy handkerchief. "It fell down during the meal yesterday; she told me to keep it."

"I did not know you are in the habit of receiving gifts from ladies!" Oswald grinned at Andreas and took the handkerchief, carefully folding it and putting it away. Then his gruff manner returned. "Get off with you now; it has been a long day."

Andreas stood up slowly.

"Go on!" Oswald almost barked at him. "Give an old man a break."

Andreas turned and walked out, into the courtyard, through the little gate, and into the woods. It was not yet completely dark when he got to the hut. Adela lifted her head from her wing; she must have been sleeping. Andreas lit his last remaining candle stumps. He quickly gathered all the things that he had already set aside earlier. Now came the hardest part—leaving his hut. He decided he would just make everything neat as if he would return the next day. He swept the floor. He used a rag to clean around Adela's makeshift perch. Finally, he grabbed one of the dried lavender bunches and stuck it in his satchel. Adela readily stepped onto his arm and allowed him to place her into her basket.

He took another look around. This had been his place more than any other. He could still stop what he was doing. Then he shook his head. No, he had made up his mind. He was ready. He blew out the candles and went out, carefully securing the door behind him.

Moving as quickly as he could with Adela in her basket and his satchel on his back, Andreas made his way through the woods. When he came to the small gate, which was not yet closed for the night, he waited to make sure there was nobody around and then entered the courtyard. At that moment, he heard footsteps and saw one of Count Cuno's retainers cross the yard. Andreas squeezed as close to the wall as he could, trying to stifle his breathing. Sweat trickled down his back. Then the steps receded; a doorway opened and closed.

The trader's cart stood near the stable door. Andreas quickly crossed the courtyard and scrambled into the back of the cart. Moving carefully in the dark and trying to remember the layout, Andreas made his way to the last perch in the back and began the work of installing Adela in her new temporary home.

Finally, Andreas crawled under a pile of rags and blankets in the corner. The rags smelled of bird feed, sweat, spilled ale, and other musty odors that he preferred not to identify. He was going to choke.

PART III

ON THE ROAD

On Transporting Falcons through Various Regions

"Before starting out on a long journey the bird should, for a few days, be made familiar with her hood until she either ceases her restless activities altogether or at least abandons the worst of them. She should also be handled and carried about more than if she had no journey to make."

   - Frederick von Hohenstaufen, *The Art of Falconry: Being the De Arte Venandi cum Avibus of Frederick II of Hohenstaufen*

Chapter 9

THE STINK OF THE RAGS KEPT ANDREAS AWAKE FOR A LONG time. He was squeezed as far back against the rear wall of the cart as was possible, and his whole body felt cramped. Every time he heard a noise, he was convinced that he was about to be discovered.

Andreas jerked awake, banging his head against the wooden slats of the cart as it rumbled along, shaking from side to side. He must have slept right through the morning. Ruts and bumps in the muddy road made him think wistfully of his straw pallet. So far, Adela stayed quiet. He had given her more food than he normally would. The only food he had brought for himself was a wizened winter apple from the cellar and a chunk of thick black bread. He chewed on the bread as slowly as he could. It tasted sweet and comforting.

When the cart finally stopped, Andreas was stiff, bruised, and thirsty. He heard Gemma jump off the cart. She called out, "I'll get some bread."

Richard said something to the servant, but Andreas could not make out the words. It became quiet. He waited until he could not hear any sounds from outside other than the mules snorting and swishing their tails. Carefully, he pushed back the rags and peeked out through the slats. He could not see anybody. The cart stood near a well in the shade of a linden tree in the center of a village square. The mules, as well as two sturdy-looking saddle horses, had their noses deep in the horse trough, supplied by the attached eight- cornered well.

Andreas jumped out and rushed over to the well. He drew up the wooden bucket and drank from it in hurried gulps. It tasted mossy, but he did not mind. He looked around for a place where he could relieve himself. A bush near the corner of a farmhouse at the edge of the square would have to do. When he was done, he glanced around, but did not see anybody. He ran back to the cart, grabbed the back door to climb up, and swung himself inside.

"Just where do you think you are going, boy?" The trader sat cross-legged on top of Andreas's pile of rags, his face implacable.

Andreas froze, crouching at the edge of the cart. The trader said, "Speak up!"

Andreas felt as if Count Cuno held him dangling in the air at the edge of the highest point of the castle's keep, about to drop him onto the rocks below. He could not remember what he had planned to tell the trader. Mutely, he leaned over and pulled on the rags in the corner. They fell free, revealing a flimsy tentlike structure and a disgruntled-looking peregrine falcon underneath. The trader raised himself from his sitting position, too tall to stand up straight inside the cart, and studied the falcon.

"And who is this?"

"That's Adela." Andreas's teeth had begun to chatter.

"I see. Or rather, I don't see. What is Adela doing in my cart?

What are you doing here, for that matter?"

"She is supposed to be dead." Andreas fumbled for words. "Indeed, that makes it all perfectly clear." Richard shook his head. "Now, I want you to go outside and wait until I have finished taking care of the birds. Then we'll talk."

Andreas fell more than climbed out of the cart and sat under the linden tree, winded and clammy from sweat. He heard Richard rummage around in the cart, talking to the birds in a low voice. Finally, he emerged and came over. Andreas stood up hastily.

The trader held a flask of water out to Andreas. "Here."

"Thank you," Andreas mumbled and drank from it before handing it back. Maybe the trader would give him some food before sending him back.

"Now then, kindly explain to me exactly how a dead peregrine that looks decidedly alive and quite healthy, I might add, ended up in my cart."

"Well, it's because of Ethelbert, you see." "Ethelbert? You mean Count Cuno's son?" "Yes. Oh, I don't know where to begin."

"How about at the beginning? What's your name?"

Something in the trader's tone of voice steadied Andreas. He told Richard about working in the mews and about Ethelbert's pronouncement of the death sentence for Adela. Finally, he said, "I want to take the falcon to the emperor and beg for sanctuary."

"Indeed. I applaud your imagination, but I don't think this is the time to discuss the merits of that plan. Meanwhile, why should I take you along?"

Andreas said, "I could help take care of your birds!"

The trader frowned at him. "You think you can? Let's see about that. Tell me, what are the proper times of day for feeding birds of prey?"

With a brief prayer of gratitude for Oswald's incessant instructions, Andreas responded readily, "Early in the morning and at night; of course, the amount depends on the bird's training and age. Not at midday—that's not good for their stomachs."

Richard did not comment, instead continued with his questions. "List the principal birds of prey and who is allowed to hunt with each type respectively."

This was easy. "Gyrfalcons are for kings, juvenile gyrfalcons or peregrines for princes, female peregrines for dukes, tercel peregrines for earls, buzzards for barons, saker falcons for knights, lanners for esquires, merlins for ladies, hobbies for young men and boys, goshawks for poor men, female sparrow hawks for priests, male sparrow hawks for clerks, and kestrels for knaves."

"You left out female goshawks for yeomen and cooks. Now, how do you carry a falcon properly on the hand?"

On and on, the questions came: What are the principal rules of training falcons? What do lanners like to hunt? What is the ideal coloring of a saker falcon? How does one transport birds of prey?

Andreas relaxed slightly; so far, he had managed to come up with a response to every question.

Richard's face remained expressionless. "What is the punishment meted out to a bird of prey if it offends its lord?"

"It depends on its rank and the offense. Oswald told me about a gyrfalcon being beheaded . . ." Andreas's voice faltered, and he fell silent.

"You knew all this, and still you took the risk? Why?" "I love Adela. And it is not fair that she should die."

"Fair? Well, it is not fair that you have now implicated me as well as my daughter."

Andreas hung his head. His stomach hurt. "I will take her out of the cart and go back. It's my fault. I will have to face whatever happens."

Richard shook his head. "How do you propose to carry the falcon back all the way we have come this morning? Anyway, she is officially dead, right?"

Andreas nodded helplessly.

At that point, there were steps behind them, and Andreas heard Gemma's cheerful voice. "Oh, Andreas! How did you get here?"

Witold stood right behind her, a glum expression on his face.

Richard said, "Let it be for now. Let's eat. It took you long enough. Did you get cheese to go with the bread?"

Gemma shook her head. "No, there wasn't any, but I got some cherries." She sat down next to her father and held out a loaf of dark bread. Richard broke off pieces and handed them around. Gemma looked at Andreas curiously but refrained from asking any questions. Andreas took the bread offered to him. He had a hard time swallowing. He kept waiting for Richard to tell him that it was time for him to take Adela and go.

Finally, Richard spit a cherry pit at the trunk of the linden tree and stood up. "Gemma, put the basket back and check the back door. Witold, get the buckets. Andreas, help me get the mules ready."

"When do you want me to take Adela out of the cart?" Andreas asked.

"Take her out? That falcon does not exist, as far as I am concerned. Come on, I don't have all day." Richard had already turned to the mules and was checking their harnesses and traces. "Here, this needs to be tightened; do the same on the other side."

Baffled, Andreas did as he was told. Helen snorted and snapped at him, but Andreas had handled enough recalcitrant horses to not be bothered by that.

When everything was ready, Richard said, "Hop up and sit in the front with Gemma. We have to move. I want to reach Lüneburg by the day after tomorrow."

The cart lumbered out of the village and down the road. Andreas was stunned by the turn of events that had him sitting up front in the fresh air, with Adela safe on her perch behind him. Gemma took something dark blue and woolen out of her bag. She unfolded it and picked up two long needles that poked through the loops along the edge. Holding on to the yarn that hung below, she moved the needles quickly, pulling the thread over and through the loops.

Fascinated, Andreas watched her rapid motions and listened to the clicking sounds. "What are you doing?"

Gemma glanced at him without stopping her movements. It was as if her fingers knew what they needed to do by themselves. "I am knitting. This is going to be a cap for the winter. Have you never seen this?"

"No. It's amazing. What else can you make with that?"

"Oh, anything really—stockings, blankets, scarves, whatever.

My father taught me." "Your father?"

"Sure, why not. He learned it from a Crusader. Apparently, many Crusaders learn to knit and mend on the road. And in the east, people have been knitting for ages."

Andreas tried to picture a knight sitting under a tree alongside a dusty road, with his sword leaning against his shield, and knitting a sock. He shook his head and grinned. Then he began to worry again. He glanced at Richard riding alongside the cart. "What do you think your father is going to do with me?"

"Do with you? I don't know. He usually has a plan. It is bound to be better than yours. What exactly were you planning?"

Andreas told her, briefly relating the events of the last few days.

Gemma laughed at him, "You must really like that bird! I wonder what Father has in mind for you." Andreas wondered, too.

Chapter 10

THIS WAS THE FIRST TIME THAT ANDREAS HAD EVER TRAVELED further than the neighboring estates around Castle Kragenberg. Sitting next to Gemma, he was surprised to see how busy the road was, with many people walking, some leading horses heavily laden with bags, and groups of merchants with carts and outriders as protection. When they rode behind a group of horsemen or other carts, the dust blew into their faces and seeped into everything.

Gemma tied a large kerchief around the lower portion of her face so that her nose and mouth were covered. When she noticed Andreas coughing, she pulled another kerchief out of her bag. "Here, this will help."

Andreas hesitated. If the boys at Castle Kragenberg could see him, they would laugh hysterically. Then again, he was not at Castle Kragenberg any longer. He took the kerchief. "Thanks."

The first night, they stayed in a crowded inn. Andreas was so tired that he barely noticed the grimy floor and the thin pallet on which he slept next to Witold and Richard in the men's room. Gemma stayed in a room with other women.

Andreas quickly learned the pattern of travel. He was surprised by the work it took to feed and water the mules and horses, check the cart and the wheels for any damage they might have incurred on the road, and take care of the birds every evening and every morning. The only way to keep the birds fit and healthy was to keep to a strict schedule of feeding, with enough time set aside for exercise. The routine would make the birds feel safe and comfortable. Richard had him do everything from brushing down the horses in the evening and checking their hooves to cleaning out the area around the perches in the cart. He had him rub harnesses, traces, leather hoods, and jesses with dubbin, a wax made from tallow, beeswax, and oil to keep leather soft and supple. He made him roll up bandages. He told him to learn the basics of knitting from Gemma.

After a few days of travel, there was a rest period. The first such was at the outskirts of Lüneburg. When they had settled in, Richard said, "We will take the birds out tomorrow; I want to see how you handle them."

Richard was silent and watchful as they worked together to get the birds ready. He let Andreas handle Adela without interfering. "Now take the lanner."

Andreas rapidly reviewed what he had learned from Oswald about lanners' style of hunting. While Adela, as a peregrine, favored a steep and extremely rapid stoop after circling her victim from high up in the air, lanners flew horizontally. Andreas had to adjust the way he used the lure. Aware of Richard's critical eye, Andreas swung it so that the lanner was given plenty of room to engage in horizontal pursuit. He brought her back successfully.

Richard said nothing, instead pointed at the saker.

Andreas hesitated. Then he said, "I have never handled a saker."

Richard nodded. "Good for you that you did not pretend to know more than you do. Sakers generally hunt by horizontal pursuit, though occasionally they dive. Watch me now."

On the third morning, Richard looked at Andreas and asked, "Do you know how to ride?"

"Not really. Oswald had me ride in the yard sometimes. Since I was not a page, it was not considered important," Andreas said.

"Well, it's high time that you learn. Witold, from now on you and Andreas will take turns. I need both of you to be able to handle yourself on a horse. Show Andreas how to mount."

Hesitantly, Andreas went to where Witold was holding his chestnut mare. Witold looked disgruntled. He silently pointed out where Andreas could hold on to the saddle to swing himself up and then handed him the reins. They set off down the road. For a while, they trotted along at a sedate pace, and Andreas was elated. He began to imagine riding with Adela on his arm in the emperor's train.

"Pull her up! Are you falling asleep back there?" Richard yelled at Andreas.

Startled, he pulled on the reins, narrowly avoiding a kick from Richard's horse. After that, Andreas paid more attention. By the time they stopped for the midday rest, Andreas was stiff and sore, his hands chafed from clutching the reins too hard.

It took only a few days until Andreas felt more comfortable in the saddle. His hands healed as he learned to hold the reins properly.

Now another form of work started. Richard tested his knowledge of the land and the towns they were passing through. "Brother Stefan did not teach you much geography, did he?" Richard scoffed, when Andreas showed his ignorance. "Well, let me try to fill in the gaps." Often his talk revolved around the overland trade routes from the large merchant towns in the north— Antwerp, Brugge, Hamburg, and Lübeck—to the Baltic regions and to the south.

Richard showed Andreas his boxes filled with goods such as silver from German mines and laces from the Low Countries. Other than falcons, he carried trade goods that did not require much space. "Lace transports well and fetches a fortune in the south."

Andreas found his head swimming with visions of sugar, gold, ivory, and precious stones traveling all the way from Africa, amber from the Baltic regions, silk, furs, carpets, pepper, cinnamon, and nutmeg from lands far to the east, and cotton, perfume, mirrors, lemons, and melons from the Holy Land. He was overwhelmed by this glimpse of a world far beyond the confines of Castle Kragenberg.

It would never have occurred to Andreas to think of falcons and other birds of prey as trade goods or even used as a way to pay ransom for someone taken prisoner. Such a mercenary perspective seemed much less appealing than the stories of falconry he heard from Oswald. When his thoughts wandered off in daydreams, Richard always noticed and admonished him to pay attention. It was as if Oswald, his uncle, and Matilda had joined forces and merged into a single harder, leaner, and more relentless teacher who would never let up.

Gemma laughed at him when he sat down in the cart, exhausted and relieved at the end of one of these sessions. "Father is thrilled to have another victim to teach."

"Why does he do this?"

"He used to do this with me, but there are limits to what I can do as a woman, in particular, in his business."

"You mean as a trader?"

"Well, yes, that, too." Gemma evidently did not wish to elaborate. Instead, she leaned over and looked at what he was doing. He struggled with a needle, trying to mend a leather bag. She took it out of his hand. "You are not doing that right. Let me show you."

Sometimes they spent the night under the huge thatch-covered roof of a farmhouse together with the family, servants, cattle, and chicken. They purchased fresh bread, eggs, and meat from farmers and cooked their meals in an open fire, setting the cast iron pots into the embers. Richard had a supply of precious spices, and when he was in a generous mood, he added some of these to the stew.

"What did you put into the meat today?" Andreas asked one evening, savoring the pungent flavor.

"That's cardamom. Do you like it?" Richard asked. He held up the ladle invitingly.

Andreas held out his bowl. "Yes, very much. Where does it come from?"

"Knights brought it back from the Holy Land. The Crusades had to be good for something after all."

Andreas was shocked at the levity of this comment. He and Tom had joked in private about many things, but he had never imagined that an adult would speak of the Holy Crusades in such a dismissive fashion. Silently, he concentrated on fishing succulent pieces of meat out of his bowl.

"Tell us about Barbarossa and the Kyffhäuser," Gemma said one evening. Richard had talked about the Hohenstaufen dynasty and Emperor Frederick II's grandfather Frederick I, known as Barbarossa. Gemma was making porridge with almond milk. She added a small amount of their precious sugar supply to the bubbling pot and stirred it vigorously.

"Barbarossa? Emperor Red Beard?" Richard sat leaning against a tree trunk, his legs stretched out in front of him. "You just like the name. I can see you running off with a man with a red beard."

"No, Father, really, tell us. What about that story that he didn't die and is going to come back one day?" Gemma carefully ladled the porridge into wooden bowls and dusted each with cinnamon. Then she looked at him expectantly.

Richard studied his bowl of porridge, thoughtfully stirring it with his spoon. "Barbarossa drowned in the Göoksu River in Turkish lands during the Crusade in 1190. Some claim that he did not die, but instead went to sleep in a hidden chamber underneath his castle on the Kyffhäuser hills in Thuringia. Supposedly, he sits there still at a stone table, fast asleep, with his beard having grown so long over the years that it grew through the table. Some say that he will emerge again from under the hill when the time comes. Ravens are often seen circling the hills; people say that is a sign of Barbarossa's presence."

"Well, his beard must be pretty itchy by now," Gemma said, laughing. Then she got serious. "Do you think he is going to come back?"

"I know he died in that river. The other is just a story. Beware of stories; they can acquire a life of their own, and people can use them for their own ends."

Andreas and Gemma looked puzzled, unsure of what Richard meant.

"As to the ravens"—Richard licked his spoon with evident pleasure—"I have seen them near the Kyffhäuser hills, but there are many reasons why ravens might be attracted to an area. If we pay too much attention to this sort of thing, we'll eventually be forced to decide whether or not to go to war based on bird droppings like the ancient Romans did."

Andreas was silent. He had heard that ravens flew across battlefields looking for corpses to feed on. He felt cold.

The next morning, Andreas went to fetch water for cleaning the perches and bird bowls. When he came up to the cart, carrying a bucket, he heard a resounding slap from inside.

"Stop that! Get your hands off me!" Gemma emerged out of the front of the cart, looking disheveled and upset.

Witold climbed out on the other side.

At that moment, Richard appeared and stood in front of Witold, casually blocking him. "Were you going somewhere? Well, then, I suggest that you take your things and leave." He spoke softly.

Witold glared at him sullenly. "Why should I leave? I contracted to work with you until Brixen. You owe me my pay."

Richard took out some coins from his purse. "Here, your pay for the last week. I warned you once before—touch my daughter again and you leave. Now is the time. Don't make me help you along."

Witold balled up his fists. Richard did not move, his expression implacable. Finally, Witold muttered angrily and turned back to the cart. Quickly, he grabbed his belongings.

"You will pay for this, you and your precious daughter, not to mention this young upstart with the chicken he is dragging around!" Witold cursed under his breath as he walked off.

Richard was tense as he and Andreas got the cart ready and harnessed the horses. "Let's go. Stay alert. With any luck, we will find another party of travelers on the road for company."

A few days later, close to the town of Braunschweig, Richard called a halt in a clearing in the woods, but he did not dismount. "Get some rest. I have an errand in town, and I'll look for a suitable inn for the night."

Andreas watched him ride off. "What's his errand?" he asked Gemma as he helped her to unhitch the mules.

"I can't tell you that." Gemma spoke shortly. "Come on, Helen, move!" She pulled the mule over toward a little copse of trees. Andreas wanted to ask more, but was afraid to appear pushy. For a while, they worked, getting the mules and the horse fed, watered, and settled in the shade. They shared a cold meat pasty. Gemma took down her workbasket and settled under a tree. She was not in a communicative mood.

Chapter 11

ANDREAS SAT IN THE SHADE ON THE GROUND BEHIND THE CART, listening to the sounds of birds and insects in the clearing and the woods around. They had already covered a long distance, and it seemed possible that they might reach Italy by the late winter. He had been working so hard in the last weeks that he had not had a chance to spend time with Adela by himself. It was as if she were calling to him. Gemma was absorbed in her knitting. Richard would be gone for at least another hour. There was time enough for a walk.

Quickly, he got Adela from her perch. He could not find the leather glove that he usually used, but decided that since he would not fly her, it would not matter so much. He glanced toward Gemma. All he could see was her head bent over her work. He would not be gone long. In the stillness of the afternoon, he could hear every twig break. The ground was covered with layers of fir tree needles and felt bouncy under his feet. He crossed a little brook and reached another clearing. Andreas took Adela's hood off so that she could look around.

"You know where you are going, Adela? We are going to Italy. You have to be ready." The falcon looked calm and alert. "You have to be fit and well trained when the emperor sees you." Adela shook out her wings. Then, she resumed scanning her surroundings.

Suddenly, a scream sliced through the air. Gemma! In his shock, Andreas jerked his arm as he turned to run back. Alarmed by the upheaval, Adela dragged her claws across his wrist and rose into the air, her jesses trailing in the wind. Andreas looked up despairingly and then ran as fast as he could, heedless of the brambles that tore at his tunic and scratched his face. He stumbled as he crossed the brook, and he could feel water seeping into his boots.

When he burst through the trees onto the clearing, he saw two men near the cart. A third man held Gemma who struggled furiously in his grip. Her neckerchief had come undone, and the man pulled on her tunic. Then Andreas recognized him; it was Witold. Andreas grabbed a tree branch from the ground. He struck Witold on the head and shoulders with the branch as hard as he could. The branch broke apart, spraying wood splinters around like a bursting sheaf of grain. Andreas clutched the remnant and tried to hit Witold again.

Witold let go off Gemma and turned to confront his attacker. "Ah, the chicken boy! Come on, I'll show you how to pluck a chicken!" He swung his fist and caught Andreas on the chin. Then he yelped and turned back to Gemma, cursing and yelling at her, "You will pay for this, girl!"

Gemma held one of her knitting needles like a short sword, ready to stick him again. "Don't you dare come closer!"

The other two men abandoned the cart and moved across the clearing. They chuckled as they approached. "Hey, smacked by a boy and stuck by a girl, Witold?"

Andreas desperately looked around for another branch when he heard the sound of hooves pounding through the forest. The two men stopped in their tracks. Witold was oblivious. He tried to grab Gemma again, and Andreas heard her tunic rip. Richard burst through the trees, his horse moving faster than Andreas had thought possible. He had drawn his sword. Pulling up his horse at the last minute, he bent down and smacked Witold across the shoulders with the flat side of the sword. The other two had already taken off as fast as they could.

Richard dismounted, tossed the reins to Andreas, and stood over Witold, crouching on the ground. "You worked for me for two years. That's the only reason why I won't kill you now. Go, and never come into my sight again."

Witold looked up at Richard with loathing and misery. Andreas saw his stringy hair, dirty clothes, and pasty skin, and felt a curious pity mixed with revulsion. Witold rose stiffly and walked off, calling to his companions to wait for him.

Richard turned to Gemma. "Are you all right?"

"Yes, Father, I am fine, really." Gemma was already pinning

her hair back under her cap and brushing off her tunic. "Andreas rushed out of the woods with a big branch and hit Witold just in time."

Richard glanced at Andreas with raised eyebrows. "You were not right here?"

Andreas flushed. "I . . ." He could not go on. "Well, speak up!"

"I went to the clearing with Adela. I wanted to take her out." Andreas looked at Richard's stern face and gulped. "I am sorry. And I lost Adela."

Richard frowned. Then he said curtly, "Let's look for her. Gemma, come along. I don't think they will come back, but it's better if we stick together." He turned and tied his horse to a tree. Then he hopped into the back of the cart and came back out with a lure and some feed. "Which way did you go?"

Numbly, Andreas pointed, and Richard quickly led them in that direction until they reached the clearing. Richard took out the lure and swung it in wide circles, while producing a high-pitched whistling sound at regular intervals, almost like the screeching mating calls of falcons. Watching Richard's calm and patient movements, Andreas felt a stirring of hope. But after nothing happened for a while, he gave up. He sat down in the grass and held his head between his hands. He tried not to cry as he thought about what Richard was going to say to him.

Suddenly, Gemma poked him in the side. "Look up," she whispered. There was Adela, circling overhead. Andreas had never seen her fly this high. Seconds later, she swooped down. She grabbed the lure and then willingly moved onto Richard's arm. He fed her immediately.

Nobody said anything on the way back to the cart. Andreas's hand and wrist burned. Trying not to draw attention to himself, he pulled up the sleeve. An angry-looking threepronged wound spread across the back of the hand and the wrist; it had bled copiously onto the sleeve.

At the campsite, Richard said, "Gemma, would you start getting things ready? We need to get to the inn before dark." Then he turned to Andreas. "Sit down over there." He pointed at the ground and then reached into the cart and rummaged around.

Carrying a bottle and a few clean rags, he knelt next to Andreas and said, "Show me your hand."

Andreas held it out, wincing. Before he knew what happened, Richard had poured some of the clear liquid from the flask over his hand. It stung so much that Andreas felt tears well up. Richard applied a salve to the wound before wrapping it up.

When Richard was done, he sat back on his heels and looked at Andreas. "I will say this one time and one time only. You know that you were wrong to go off like that. You cannot act as if you were alone. If you had not tried to defend Gemma the way you did, you would now be walking back to Castle Kragenberg." He stood up. "Let's go."

Shaken and uncomfortable, Andreas was afraid to look at Gemma. He fumbled with the saddle and winced when he had to use his hand to tighten the cinch. Gemma led the mules to the cart, and Richard helped her to get everything ready before mounting his horse.

Riding alongside the cart, Richard glanced at Andreas and said drily, "You will have a fine scar to remind you of this day for the rest of your life."

It was evening by the time they reached the inn. Andreas had a hard time sleeping the first night after the attack. His hand hurt, and he could not stop thinking about what he had done. In the morning, Richard insisted on pouring more of the foul burning liquid on Andreas's wound.

"Why do you do that?" Andreas asked curiously. "It stings." "Good. That means it is working. I got it from a monastery. I

learned that on the Crusade—if you don't keep wounds clean, you can die. Admittedly, many knights preferred to drink the stuff rather than pour it over their wounds."

They stayed at the inn for several days. Richard appeared to know several people, talking to them over pitchers of ale in a dark corner of the common room. Twice he disappeared for a few hours.

Andreas was grateful for Gemma's cheerful company. She never said anything about what happened in the woods. Occasionally, she checked his wound, helping him to keep it clean and treat it with the salve Richard had used. It itched as it healed.

Whenever Andreas moved his hand, the skin pulled.

As they traveled further south, Richard added a new element to their evening program in the villages where they stayed overnight. Andreas noticed how the cheerfully painted cart deflected people's mistrust and nervousness around strangers. After they had settled in and taken care of the mules, horses, and falcons, Richard took out a large leather bag. He walked to the village green and proceeded to entertain the villagers. He had juggling balls made of wood, others made of yarn and leather, and a wooden box, which he used to perform disappearing tricks. Gemma assisted him, juggling with enthusiasm and great skill. The villagers crowded around, delighted by the entertainment.

Often one of the villagers invited them to share a meal with his family. Andreas was intrigued by Richard's quiet way of asking questions in a manner that conveyed genuine interest in everything without appearing nosy. People complained about the emperor, the dues that they had to pay to their lord, the insecurity, the bad weather destroying the harvest, and thieves. Gemma chatted to the women; they told her about children dying from mysterious illnesses, food shortages, and wild boars from the manorial woods getting into their fields.

One morning, when they were back on the road, Andreas screwed up his courage and asked, "Why do you do this— juggling, performing tricks, and all the talking? I thought you were a trader."

"What is your idea of a trader? Someone carrying around sacks full of flour or seeds? You can trade in all sorts of things— even entertainment and news." Richard guided his horse around a bad rut in the road. "Let's move. At this rate we will never get over the Alps before the spring."

Andreas knew that he would not find out anything else that day.

Chapter 12

A FEW DAYS LATER, THEY REACHED GOSLAR.

The porter at the town gate looked bored. "What kind of a cart is this? Didn't you have enough of one color to paint the whole cart?" He chuckled and then walked around the cart to determine its approximate weight and type. "What are you carrying, anyway? Where are your trading papers?"

Richard handed over a rolled-up document indicating his trading status. He looked at the porter haughtily. "I find that your tone leaves a lot to be desired. What happened to basic courtesy in the town of Goslar?"

"Hey, you want courtesy? You better go on to the castle on the hill. Though from what I hear, they might just kick you down the hill and out of town. Courtesy is getting rare these days. We just have to make do with tolls." The man spat on the ground. "You will pay the rate for a two-wheeler."

Richard held out a few coins. The man grunted and disappeared in his gatehouse.

Once they had settled Gemma in the common room at the inn, Richard bade Andreas to follow him.

Richard walked quickly, so that Andreas did not get any opportunity to ask questions. He marveled at the signs above doorways indicating a butcher, an apothecary, a tile maker, and many others. Andreas counted at least five shops selling fabrics and offering tailoring work within a few blocks from one another; there were several cobblers in one street and hat makers in another. He stumbled over a pile of excrement. After that, he picked his way more carefully.

As they came around one street corner, Andreas heard a screeching noise from above and looked up just in time to see a woman toss the contents of a chamber pot onto the road as a man stumbled out of the doorway. "That will teach you to come home dead drunk!" she screamed at the man, who ducked just in time and then walked off without responding.

Richard glanced back and grinned at Andreas.

They reached a little square in front of a church; the lane led up an incline to a gate with a castle behind. Richard stopped in the shade of a tree.

"Now you need to know a little bit more about what I am doing. I told you that there are other things to trade in beyond falcons and cloth. Occasionally, I carry messages."

Suddenly, a lot of little things that Andreas had noticed throughout the last weeks made sense. "You are gathering information as well, aren't you?"

"Ah, someone has been paying attention. You're right. I am part of a large network of people carrying messages and gathering information for the emperor. It's time for you to start making yourself useful. Consider this your first training exercise. Here, take this envelope." Richard reached into his breast shirt and pulled out a packet wrapped in oiled parchment. The red sealing wax displayed the coat of arms of Lüneburg, a dancing lion surrounded by hearts. "Hide it in your hose. Go inside and find the castellan. His name is Master Anton. I leave it up to your imagination how you will be permitted to see him. Tell him that the falcon trader sent you and give him this packet. Don't give the envelope to anybody else."

Andreas was puzzled. "But Goslar is an imperial city. Why is this necessary?"

"Even in Goslar, it is a good idea to exercise discretion."

Andreas gaped at Richard. He wished he could have told Tom about this. After a moment, he asked, "How will I know that I am speaking to Master Anton?"

"Ah, good question. He will expect a password from you and he has to give you his." Richard glanced around and then spoke the passwords softly. "I will wait for you underneath the beech in front of the church." Then he clapped Andreas on the back. "Well, go on."

Andreas kept repeating the passwords as he walked into the courtyard. Through an open doorway, he saw a bustle of activity that reminded him of Matilda's kitchen, albeit on a grander scale.

A servant came around the corner, jostling his arm. "Who are you? What do you want?"

Andreas looked at the young woman's overheated and disgruntled face and took in her arm and wrist, red and raw. "That must hurt! Did you burn it?"

Mollified, she answered, "Yes, I got burned by steam. I never knew steam could do so much damage."

Andreas grimaced; it was as if he could feel the stinging on his own skin. He wished he could remember what was in the salve Matilda used when this happened at Castle Kragenberg.

"What do you want? I can't stand around here all day," the young woman said impatiently.

"Oh, sorry." Andreas shook his head, embarrassed. "I need to see Master Anton. Do you know where I can find him?" he said.

"Master Anton? He is in the great hall. What do you want from him?"

"My aunt asked me to give him a message." "Your aunt?"

"Yes, Aunt Matilda," Andreas said disingenuously, silently apologizing to Matilda. Trying to adopt the pose of a dull-witted boy, he scratched his nose and smiled vacantly.

"Oh well. Just go on through there."

Following the young woman's directions, Andreas walked into the great hall. A short hunchbacked man stood in front of a large board, two apprehensive-looking servants next to him. He was waving his hands. "No, no, this is not right! Remember the saltcellar always goes here, to the right of the lord. Where is the wine?" He glanced around and noticed Andreas. "Who are you? Can't you see that I am busy?"

"The falcon trader sent me," Andreas said.

"Oh?" The hunchback nodded to the two servants to carry on and walked toward Andreas. "Does he have any falcons for my lord?"

"No, only goshawks and buzzards."

By now, the castellan stood quite close to Andreas. "What a pity. We were hoping for a peregrine!" He lowered his voice. "Do you have anything for me?"

Andreas nodded and began to reach under his tunic to pull out the packet, when the castellan frowned at him, shaking his head, and said softly, "Wait for me in the hallway."

Speaking loudly, he said, "Well, better luck next time. Go on to the kitchen and let them give you a honey cake to take along." He pointed at the hallway.

Andreas did as he was told. The hallway was long, and he felt uncomfortable standing there in the fragmented light from a mullioned window. Somebody would come up to him any minute, asking him what he was doing there. Just then, the castellan came out from another doorway down the hall.

"Well, give me what you have."

Relieved, Andreas handed over his packet.

"Here, this is for your master," the castellan said, handing Andreas another packet and a heavy little felt bag.

By the time Andreas had made his way outside and back to the little square in front of the church, he was lightheaded with excitement. Richard was already there. "Ah, I see that you were successful. Did Master Anton give you anything for me?" Andreas reached inside his tunic and pulled out the little packet and the felt bag. "Yes, here."

"Well done. Now let's get back to the inn."

The next weeks passed in a blur. Richard set a steady pace. Throughout, he continued barraging Andreas with information, quizzing him about everything he learned, and occasionally dispatching him with messages.

When they reached Bamberg, Richard chose an inn just outside the city wall. After having assured himself that Gemma was comfortable, he said, "Come along, Andreas. I need to see my banker."

Together they walked toward the center of the town. They stopped at a house that had a plaque above the doorway showing three golden balls suspended from a bar. When Andreas pointed at it, Richard said, "That's the sign of a money lender and banker."

Inside, a frail elderly man sat at a table covered with ledgers. Peering at Richard with tired eyes, he opened one of the ledgers and had Richard sign at a spot indicated. With a sigh, he opened a strong box. He counted out coins and poured the final amount into a leather bag that Richard had brought along.

"You'd think that poor banker is being robbed blind every single day," Richard said when they were back outside. He bought a small meat pie for each of them from a market stall. It was still warm and tasted delicious. When they came onto the central square, Andreas stopped in his tracks. In front of him was the largest building he had ever seen. Its four huge towers had pointed roofs that seemed to stretch themselves impossibly high into the sky. In addition to the cross over the central arch, there was a cross on each of the towers.

"That's a church?"

"That is a cathedral." Richard responded as he led him inside. Sounds reverberated in the vast, cool space, and it smelled of candle wax and incense. Richard genuflected and knelt quietly on the flagstones for a few moments. Andreas knelt next to him, uncomfortably aware of not having gone to confession for a long time. On their way out, they passed two marble tombs in a side nave.

"Who is buried here?" Andreas whispered.

"That's Emperor Henry II and his wife, Empress Cunigunde."
"And that?" Andreas pointed at a monumental statue at the north pillar of the choir. It was a knight on a horse, and he wore a crown. His expression was remote and abstracted as if his thoughts were far away.

"Emperor Frederick."

Andreas stepped closer. Puzzled, he looked at the stone carving beneath the horse's hooves. At first glance, it looked like a thicket. Then he realized there was a face carved into the dense tangle of leaves, a face out of another world, with deep-set eyes, a full mouth, and a nose with wide nostrils.

Richard said, "That's the Green Man. He represents life and rebirth."

The next day, they continued south. Richard was anxious to make it across the Alps before snow made passage impossible.

Every morning, they were up at first light, and rest periods were short. Andreas was awed by the approaching mountains. They were larger than anything he ever imagined.

Richard pointed at one of them. "See that mountaintop? That's the Habicht, which means 'hawk.' Isn't it beautiful?"

"Beautiful" seemed an odd word for a landscape so huge and unforgiving, with snow along the rocky slopes and mountain peaks as far the eye could see.

"How do we get across these mountains with the cart?" Andreas asked curiously.

"We will use the Brenner Pass. It's by the far the best route across. The Romans built this one as well as another earlier one that crosses the Alps at a higher point," Richard said.

They stopped overnight with a dairy farmer. They slept in the hayloft, lulled by the snuffling and occasional soft mooing of the cows.

In the middle of the night, Andreas woke up feeling sick. Trying not wake Richard and Gemma, he climbed down the ladder. He barely made it outside and threw up in the mud next to the barn door. Back in the hayloft, he shivered for a long time before dropping off to sleep.

In the morning, they reached the high point of the Brenner Pass and began their descent toward Italy. It was windy, and the air smelled of snow. Andreas kept thinking about the serene face of the horseman in Bamberg, cool and unearthly, above the vivid face of the Green Man, ready to burst forth out of his wilderness. His head ached. The snow along the slopes was blinding.

"Watch out!" Richard grabbed the reins of his horse and pulled him sideways. "You almost went down the slope! What's the matter with you?"

Andreas shook his head trying to clear the confusion.

Richard pulled up his horse and dismounted, signaling to Gemma to stop the cart. He walked over to Andreas. "Give me your hand."

Andreas found his hand held in a cool firm grip.

Richard said, "You are burning up. How long have you been feeling like this?"

"I don't know," Andreas mumbled. How odd, the mountains appeared to sway in the wind.

Richard cursed softly. He pulled a flask out of his saddle pack. "Here, have a few sips of this. It might tide you over."

Andreas swallowed. It hurt his throat as it went down. Then a glow spread out from his stomach. He handed the flask back, and Richard remounted.

The next few hours went by in a blur. Whenever he closed his eyes, the Green Man appeared, first straddling the Habicht and tossing huge avalanches in all directions, then standing over Adela with a sword raised high in the air. Swinging the sword downward, the Green Man turned into Ethelbert who screamed at Andreas, "You stole my falcon!"

At one point, Richard moved around him, doing something to the saddle. Then Andreas ceased noticing anything.

Low voices woke him up. Richard grabbed him and pulled him off the horse.

"Come along. Let's get you inside." Andreas stumbled into a small room.

"Here, sit down." Hands pushed him onto a pallet and pulled off his tunic. Andreas began shivering again. A soft blanket dropped down like cloud, and he closed his eyes.

PART IV

OVER THE MOUNTAINS

On the Improper Handling of Falcons

"A bad temper is a grave failing. A falcon may frequently commit acts that provoke the anger of her keeper, and unless he has his anger strictly under control, he may indulge in improper acts toward a sensitive bird so that she will very soon be ruined. Laziness and neglect in an art that requires so much work and attention are absolutely prohibited."

- Frederick von Hohenstaufen, *The Art of Falconry: Being the De Arte Venandi cum Avibus of Frederick II of Hohenstaufen*

Chapter 13

IT WAS HOT. ANDREAS TRIED TO TAKE OFF HIS TUNIC, BUT HIS arms were entangled in the string from Adela's lure. The string had wrapped itself around his throat so he could hardly breathe. Desperately, he lurched from side to side, groping for the reins to control his horse. A firestorm rolled down the mountainside. Hundreds of ravens flew in and out of the flames. A gyrfalcon with glowing red eyes and its wings on fire swooped down on Andreas and covered him completely. Then everything stopped.

Andreas woke up. He tried to move, but something warm and damp constrained him. He was in a dark room, illuminated only by a fire in the hearth and a candle on the table. A man sat at the table, his head bent over a manuscript. He turned around and looked at Andreas.

"Ah, you are awake. How are you doing?"

Andreas tried to answer, but found that his throat was too dry. The man came over and laid a hand on his forehead. "Good, the wrap worked. It's time to take it off." He pulled damp rags away from Andreas's body and wiped his sweaty face. Then he covered Andreas with a soft, heavy blanket.

Andreas whispered, "Where am I?"

The man turned to the table and filled a cup with water from a jug. He crouched next to Andreas and held the cup to his lips. "You are safe. You have been very sick. Richard and Gemma went to Bressanone."

Andreas took a few sips from the cup. He was mesmerized by the man's deep voice. It flowed all around him like a warm wave and made him think of monks singing in the abbey church near Castle Kragenberg. His intonation was odd, as if he was not used to speaking German.

"Bressanone?"

The man smiled at him. "Oh, yes, you call it Brixen. It is about a day's travel from here."

"Are they coming back?" Andreas asked, oddly disengaged. Everything that had happened to him over the past months seemed to have faded into the distance. He moved his hands under the blanket, relaxed and empty of thought.

"Richard and Gemma? Certainly. They will be back in a few weeks when you are ready to travel again."

"And Adela?" Andreas croaked.

"Your falcon is fine. She and the others are in my little stable. My goat and my donkey are none too happy about it, but they are all warm and comfortable."

Satisfied, Andreas closed his eyes.

When Andreas woke up again, light came into the room through cracks in the window shutter. Embers from a dying fire glowed in the hearth. Andreas watched them wink, shift shape, and collapse into themselves. His nose itched, and he pulled up his arm to scratch it. His hand touched something that felt like the back of an unshorn sheep. He squinted and realized that it was a blanket made out of sheepskin. The leather had been cured so that it was soft and smooth, and the woolly side was turned toward his body. It was warm and cozy.

The man sat at a table in the corner of the room. He slept with his head leaning on the surface. A candle had burned down to the stump. Crockery and pots competed for space with piles of paper, an ink jar, and quills. A shelf was filled to overflowing with vials, jars, and little burlap bags. A set of light-colored pipes, strung up in a row and arranged in an ascending order, lay on top of the pile of logs next to the hearth. Andreas studied it in bemusement, when he felt something move next to his legs. He saw two eyes peering at him from the foot of his pallet. Andreas stared back, and the eyes shifted. A small gray cat stretched itself, curling and uncurling the claws on its white front paws, and then put its head down, rolling itself into a ball with a contented sigh.

The man at the table raised his head and looked at Andreas. "Good morning." He stood up and placed wood on the fire.

Andreas rubbed his eyes and sat up. He was lightheaded, but no longer dizzy.

The man held out a washrag. "I see that Egon approves of you. Consider it an honor. He usually hides from all visitors."

Andreas took the proffered rag, wiping it over his face and neck. When he tried to stand, he wobbled, but the man took his arm and steadied him. He supported Andreas to the privy outside. It was windy. Vast banks of early morning fog swept down from the mountains and rolled into the valley below. Andreas could just make out the beginning of the road south and behind the tiny homestead, the tall fir trees hugging the mountainside.

Nicholas looked at the sky. "More snow coming. It will be a while before Richard and Gemma get back. Do you want to see Adela?"

"Oh yes, please."

The birds were in a small stable behind the house. It smelled of goat and donkey. Richard had brought the perches from the cart into the shed. The birds were sleeping. Andreas could see only the gray brown feathers on Adela's back, her beak tucked into her plumage and the feathers fluffed out for warmth.

"Satisfied? Let's go back inside." Nicholas grasped Andreas's arm and gently steered him back to the house. The wind almost tore the door out of his hand, and he secured it with an iron bolt once they were inside.

"Here, sit at the table." He poured water from a kettle into a mug and placed it next to Andreas.

Andreas sipped the fragrant brew gratefully. It tasted like chamomile. "What is your name?"

"Oh, sorry, I guess we were never introduced." The man smiled at Andreas. "My name is Nicholas. I am a friend of Richard."

"What were the wet rags for?" Andreas asked. Things were coming back to him.

"It's to make you sweat and drive out the sickness. Anyway, today there will be no visitors, and you can rest."

Andreas nodded. Gratefully, he returned to the pallet and sat down, trembling from the exertion.

Andreas slept most of the day. Once when he woke up, he found that Nicholas had placed a mug with water and a hunk of bread next to his pallet. Later that day, there was a bowl filled with lentil stew. It was peaceful and quiet, and he slept.

88

Chapter 14

THE NEXT DAY, ANDREAS FELT BETTER. NICHOLAS LEFT HIM alone, saying that he had to go to the village. Andreas went to the shed to check on Adela and the others. They looked healthy and were eating well. The rest of the time he sat on his pallet. With needle and thread, he mended some of the jesses. He did not have Gemma's skill with a needle. Irritably, he tried to work it back and forth through the leather. Having time to think was not soothing. His plan seemed as nonsensical and foolish as the unfinished gazebo at Castle Kragenberg. Even Adela had become blurry in his mind, almost like a speck in the sky, flying higher and higher until she was gone. Frustrated, he twisted and pulled on the leather strip.

On the third day, Nicholas said, "Today, I have people coming here to see me." Without any further comment, he cleaned off the table, moving some of the crockery out of the way. Then he set out piles of linen rags and strips, together with various jars and curious- looking implements.

"What are you doing? Why do people come to see you?" Before Nicholas could respond, there was a knock on the door.

Nicholas opened up and admitted an old shepherd. He was wrapped in a large, blanket-style tunic from which snow dripped onto the floorboards. Andreas could only see his shaggy head and beard. "Good morning, Signor Nico. My knee has been hurting again.

It has gotten so I can tell when snow is coming. It keeps me up at night." His voice was scratchy like someone who sat at too many smoky fires.

"Sit down, Ranald. Let's take a look." Nicholas pointed at the bench.

Groaning a little, the man sat on the bench and pulled up his tunic. Nicholas ran his hand over the swollen knee. Then he handed the man a salve. "Here, rub this on your knee tonight and over the next few days. Keep it warm and dry if you can."

The shepherd stood up and reached into his satchel. "I brought a few fresh eggs for you and a loaf of bread that the wife made."

"Thank you, Ranald."

This was the first of several visitors that day. One needed a remedy for his cough, one complained about pain in the back, and a mother brought in her sons who had bad cuts on their faces from fighting. Nicholas sewed up the gashes with a needle and thread. Most brought something for him—eggs, cured meat, flour, barley, honey, even some homespun linen.

Andreas watched, fascinated and absorbed. He was surprised when Nicholas said, "That should be the last one for the day."

The day after, three men appeared at Nicholas's door. Two supported a third one between them. He had fallen into a crevasse while trying to retrieve a mule. His hands were a raw soggy mess from the branches he had tried to hold on to on his way down. His tunic and hose were covered in caked blood, and he was barely conscious. His leg was broken. Nicholas took one look and said to Andreas, "I could use your help."

Nicholas told Andreas to clear the table and set water to boil. Nicholas showed Andreas how to bathe the wounds and how to place stitches on the deeper cuts. Together they straightened out the leg and splinted it. Nicholas gently touched the man's rib cage, and he flinched. Ruefully, Nicholas said, "I think you broke a few ribs. It will hurt for a while; there is not much I can do about it." But he wrapped a long bandage around the man's torso. "That might help a bit."

Finally, Nicholas turned to the two companions who had been silently watching all the while. "You should leave your friend here, until he is no longer dizzy. He can sleep on a spare pallet. Come back with a stretcher in two days."

Andreas went outside to watch the men make their way down the trail. It was already late in the afternoon. He had lost track of time.

Nicholas appeared next to him and draped his arm around Andreas's shoulders. "Well done."

After that, Nicholas had Andreas assist him often. He

explained what he did and what herbs and other remedies he used. This became the pattern of their days.

Every few days, they went to the village together. Andreas relished the clean air the first time that they walked down the trail toward the village nestled at the foot of the mountains. "What are those tall dark green trees?" he asked Nicholas.

"Those are cypresses. You will see more of those when you get down into the Po valley and Tuscany." They reached the main square. It was market day; farmers were selling cheeses, meats, bread, cabbages, and other winter vegetables, and jars of olive oil and wine.

A woman called out as they walked, "Ah, Signor Nico, how are you doing?"

Nicholas gave her a warm smile. "Signora Pizzini, I am very well. How is your family?"

"Oh, thank you! All is well. Just the little one, my Magda, keeps having problems with her ears."

"Bring her to me soon. Maybe I can help. Remember to have her cover her head with a scarf."

That day, Nicholas, with Andreas in tow, called on a number of people throughout the village, checking on them, admonishing and giving advice. Finally, they walked home, carrying a bag filled with bread, dried lentils, salted ham, and a hard cheese.

In the evenings, they talked, while Nicholas measured out herbs and poured them into little linen pouches.

"Matilda, the cook at Castle Kragenberg, used herbs for healing, but you have so many more. Did you study medicine?" Andreas asked one evening.

"Oh, I wish. Sadly, I know very little. The most important one I only learned over time—healing takes patience and hard work. There are no shortcuts." Nicholas got up and took a big manuscript from the shelf. "Here, take a look."

Andreas opened it. He had never held a big manuscript like this in his hands. "How did you get it?" he asked.

"I got it from a man who had robbed a monastery. At that time, I thought I would sell it somewhere. Later, I was ashamed to have it and hid it in my bag; I did not know from which monastery it had been taken. I really only looked at it here. It was almost as if I was meant to have it."

Andreas opened the manuscript to the first page. He read the title out loud, *"Practical Medicine According to Trotula."* He looked up. "Who was Trotula?"

"She was a physician who worked in Salerno and wrote several treatises like this. I know that there are other books like that, but regrettably I never saw any of them."

Andreas was awed by this idea of entire books about medicine. At Castle Kragenberg, people who got sick usually went to Matilda. The monk in charge of the infirmary at the abbey came when one of the knights or Count Cuno was sick. Sometimes it had seemed to him that the care and treatment of hunting birds was more sophisticated than that of people. This book pointed at a world of knowledge far beyond anything he could have imagined. Andreas had never heard of many of the ailments she discussed, much less known that there might be remedies for any of them. Regretfully, Andreas handed the manuscript back and watched Nicholas carefully place it back on the shelf.

Thereafter, Nicholas took it out regularly, and together they looked at the different sections and studied the sketches. The illustrations were finer than many he had seen when his uncle had shown him manuscripts at the abbey.

"What is that?" Andreas pointed to an image of a man surrounded by the signs of the zodiac.

"I am not sure. I think that there is a link between astrological signs and health."

Andreas looked at the crab, the bull, the twins, and others doubtfully. "And this?" The next image showed a human figure divided into four quarters.

"Those are the four humors. Trotula talks about it here." Nicholas turned the page and pointed. "I don't understand this very well."

Andreas had already forgotten about the humors. Intently, he studied a drawing of the body that showed the bones and the internal organs. "It's funny. This one makes me think of a building, with openings for things coming in and going out, and a foundation structure."

Nicholas smiled at him. "I never thought of it like that.

Certainly, if you take one or two of the elements away, the whole structure collapses."

"What's that?" Andreas pointed to a sketch of a man with a deep incision in his side and a skinny tube sticking out at the lower end of the incision, pointing downward.

"I think that's supposed to help drain pus from a wound. I don't quite know how it works. But I did learn not to close deep wounds completely and to leave an opening on the lower end, until it begins to heal."

A large portion of the manuscript dealt with illnesses of women. "Some of this might well have helped my mother," Andreas said wistfully.

"Perhaps. Sometimes there is nothing that can be done."

Andreas did not look at him. "My mother is dead." Then he added abruptly, "My father is probably dead, too. I never knew him. He disappeared before I was born."

Nicholas nodded, but did not comment. He rummaged in his box and brought out a wooden board. "Do you know how to play chess?"

"No. How did you get a chess set?"

"A knight gave to me in gratitude after I did him a small service once."

Nicholas set up the figures and explained them to Andreas. At first, it seemed easy, but soon Andreas realized that this was one of the most challenging games he had ever played. He lost three games in rapid succession. After that, they played often.

"How did you come to be here?" Andreas asked one evening. The moment the words were out of his mouth, he wanted to take them back. "I am sorry; I have no right to ask that."

"It's all right," Nicholas said. "It was a long time ago, and I don't mind telling you. It's the same old story of a young man who loses his love and wanders through the world." Nicholas smiled at Andreas as if mocking himself. "That's the short version. The longer version is a bit more complicated." His accent gradually became less pronounced as if he was getting used to speaking German again. "I was going to become a sculptor. I dreamed of carving altarpieces. At least that was a plan when I was young."

"What happened?"

"I guess I did not really want it all that much. I wasted many years of my life." His voice held a bitterness that Andreas had not heard before. After a pause, he continued. "I once loved a young woman with all my heart. I met Katrina when I came back from the Crusade in 1229. Her parents had not welcomed my suit, since I had nothing to support her with. We were going to go before a priest. Then something happened. I got into a fight with someone and lost my temper. I killed him. I could not go home." Nicholas looked at the fire in the hearth.

"So what did you do?" Andreas asked.

Nicholas sighed. "What could I do? I did not know anything other than fighting. My skill with wood carving was hardly likely to feed me. I did odd jobs here and there. I begged. Eventually, I joined up with a band of mercenaries. We worked for anybody who was willing to pay for our services. My good fortune was to get badly hurt near here. An old woman healer took me in and took care of me. This house was her house. She taught me everything I know about healing. Of course, I never studied any of this properly. On the other hand, the people here have no one else."

Chapter 15

ONE AFTERNOON, WHEN ANDREAS CAME BACK FROM THE SHED after checking on the birds, he looked at the sky. The light had changed, and it felt like spring. He missed Richard and Gemma. As soon as this thought occurred to him, he realized that he would have to leave Nicholas. There would be no more reading in Trotula's manuscript, no more talking about the healing properties of herbs. Just yesterday, Nicholas had shown him how to stitch up a bad cut in a young shepherd's hand. The shepherd had smiled at Andreas when he was done. Slowly, he went back inside.

Nicholas was banking the fire in the hearth. He looked up when he heard Andreas and said, "I need to go into the woods to get some kindling. Do you want to come?"

Andreas nodded.

"Good. We will take the donkey along."

It was a dry, sunny day. The sun had melted most of the snow, leaving glittering patches here and there in the bushes. The mountains looked like a giant's messy treasure trove of roughly hewn crystals, with dark slashes along the sides where the snow cover had blown away. The donkey carried two large baskets, gently bouncing on his sides. Following a small trail, they went into a forest of fir trees. The ground was littered with needles, cones, and dry branches. Occasionally, clumps of snow dropped off the swaying treetops. Eventually, Nicholas stopped and tied the donkey to a tree. Then they began to gather kindling.

When they had filled the baskets, they sat on a tree trunk. Through an opening in the line of trees, Andreas looked into the valley below. Nicholas pulled something out of his satchel. It was the odd set of pipes that Andreas had seen in the house.

"What is that?"

"A pan flute." Nicholas held it to his lips and began to blow into the pipes.

It produced the eeriest sounds Andreas had ever heard. It made him think of damp forest floors, water spilling over boulders, and wood ducks calling from among the reeds. Then it became apparent that Nicholas had merely been warming up. Taking a deep breath, he launched into a tune that made Andreas want to jump up and sing and shout. The notes seemed to dance among the trees and leap up into the clouds.

After a brief pause, Nicholas started up again, playing a softly plaintive, dark melody, full of longing.

Andreas listened with his teeth sunk into his lip, staring into the valley below. It was as if the music evoked all his jumbled thoughts. He wanted to watch Adela soar above the scudding wisps of clouds and to ride with a falcon on his arm; he wanted to puzzle out the beauty and mystery of the human body and to feel again and again the bewitching sense of being able to help and to heal. He felt split, torn by his dreams, and he could not see the road ahead. He wished he could once again lie in his bed, waiting for his mother's soft lavender-scented hand caressing his cheek.

After a last drawn-out note, Nicholas stopped.

Andreas rubbed his hands over his face. "I cannot remember my mother's face."

He had never told anyone this before. He thought of his feeling of dread when he heard her cough through the night. For a long time after she died, all Andreas could think about was the smell of sickness and the rasping sounds of her breathing. Only much later, he could once again recall his mother's shock of blond hair, when it was not pinned up in the morning, her slender hands sewing, and her voice filled with laughter when she told him a story.

Nicholas said gently, "You know I cannot remember Katrina's face? But when I play music, it is as if she is right there."

Andreas nodded. Then he looked down and saw that the flute had fallen on the ground. He picked it up. "Would you show me how to play this?"

"It's not that difficult. You just have to keep working on it. Let me show you how to blow into the pipes."

After several tries, Andreas was able to produce a few reedy notes. Out of breath and red in the face from the effort, he grinned at Nicholas and said, "This sounds like the squealing door in the great hall at Castle Kragenberg!"

"You are working too hard at it. Relax your lips a bit. It gets easier." Nicholas stood up. "We should head back now."

By the time they reached the house, it had turned chilly. Andreas helped Nicholas store the kindling in the shed.

Nicholas looked at the darkening sky. "We might get some snow flurries tonight. Come, I will make us something hot to drink."

They sat at the table, warmed by the fire in the hearth. Andreas blew on his mug, and the steam rose around his face. The wind swept around the little house, and Andreas thought of the sheepskin blanket on his pallet. He ran his hand over the table's rough surface, notched here and there with burn marks and with spots where ink had spilled or the quill slipped.

"I wish I could stay here," he blurted out. "I want to learn more about healing."

Nicholas got up and put another log on the fire. Then he turned back to the table and began to set up the chessboard. "I can always find a straw pallet for you," he said, intent on arranging the chess figures.

Feeling obscurely rejected by this offhand remark, Andreas did not respond. They played silently.

That evening, Andreas, for the first time, was able to defeat Nicholas. Andreas positioned his queen and his bishop in such a way that Nicholas's king could not move out of check.

"Checkmate!"

Nicholas tipped his king over in acceptance of his defeat and smiled at Andreas, with a curiously sad and wistful expression on his face. Then he stood up to bank the fire.

"Let's go fly the birds tomorrow," he said. "It will be a clear day, with just a bit of snow on the ground—perfect for hunting. That lot in the shed needs some exercise. They have been cooped up too long."

Early the next morning, they went to the shed. Nicholas lent his assistance, but for the most part seemed content to watch Andreas get the birds ready. It was a sunny, breezy day. The peaks of the Alps seemed very far away, indistinct against the horizon.

"If you can see them clearly, chances are that the weather is changing," Nicholas said, leading the way along a mountain trail to a clearing. "It has been a mild winter."

Since the birds had not been out for a while, Andreas decided to fly them to the lure only. The birds were sluggish and uninterested until the cold air woke them up. Andreas found it hard to pay attention, fascinated by the landscape and distracted by his thoughts.

He swung the lure for the merlin, a trim little female, buff and brown all over. The smallest of the birds, it was sometimes called a pigeon hawk because it resembled a pigeon in flight. But it was fast and aggressive. Andreas's thoughts wandered. The merlin, perhaps sensing the lack of focus in the circles of the lure, veered off. With his heart in his throat, Andreas watched the bird swoop down into the valley below. By the time he realized what the bird was hunting, it was over. To his relief, the merlin willingly returned to the lure, carrying her prize, a white-winged snowfinch. Andreas marveled at the merlin's ability to spy out the little bird, whose drab brown and white coloring made it nearly invisible in the winter landscape.

With shaking fingers, he secured the merlin and covered her head with the hood. He could not begin to imagine what Richard would have done if Andreas had lost the merlin.

Adela was restless and eager to move. She jumped up and down on Andreas's arm so that he had difficulty removing her hood. All his frustration welled up inside of him. Angrily, he jerked on her jesses. "Hold still, will you!" he yelled at the bird, reaching for her hood.

Adela shied away from his hand. Andreas flushed. He almost hoped for a sharp reprimand from Nicholas, but he said nothing. Sweating and miserable, Andreas held his arm still and talked in a low voice until he felt Adela's tension ebb away. When she was relaxed and alert, he slowly took the hood off and launched her into the air.

Adela flew as if she had not been cooped up at all, with precision, strength, and speed. Andreas watched her wheel and turn. She easily returned to the lure, calmly settling on his gloved hand and taking her reward like an empress accepting tribute. Perhaps she had forgiven him.

When they walked back to take the birds to the shed, Andreas was tired, but content. He knew now that he had to go on. He had made a choice for Adela, and he had to carry it through. Everything else would have to wait.

A grin spread over his face as he thought of what Tom might have said to him. He could just hear his soft voice that always held a hint of laughter in it. "And what about you? You can't stay holed up in this nice little house at the foot of the Alps, stuffing herbs into linen bags and playing with Egon the cat!"

Chapter 16

"ADELA IS SICK!" ANDREAS BURST INTO THE HOUSE; A GUST OF wind followed his precipitous entry.

Nicholas carefully closed the linen bag that he had been filling from a jar. Then he looked up and asked calmly, "What do you think is the matter?"

"I am not sure. Her feathers look dull. She is not eating."

"What else could help you to determine what might be going on?"

"You sound just like Oswald," Andreas said peevishly.

"Well, what did Oswald teach you about this sort of thing?"

Nicholas spoke severely and was evidently not willing to rush into the shed to see what ailed Adela.

Andreas turned around and went back to the shed. He opened one of the shutters in order to have more light. He studied the falcon. He looked at her stool to see if the color was different. That seemed to be fine. Her eyes were clear. But Adela definitely was listless.

Andreas chewed on his lower lip. Her feathers looked different. He did not like to touch her unnecessarily, remembering Oswald's stern lectures on this. "A bird of prey is not a house pet. It is a wild animal and should be allowed to remain precisely that. Her wildness is what makes her a good hunter." Reaching out slowly, he grasped a few dark gray feathers from her wing and tugged gently. They dropped easily into his hand. Disgruntled, Adela shifted around on her perch. This must be the answer. She was going into molt early. The wing feathers were always the first to come out. No wonder she looked so droopy. Normally, she would have started shedding her old coat in March or even April when there was ample food available. Andreas tried to think back. It was almost February. Amazed, he realized he had been with Nicholas for more than a month. Perhaps being cooped up so long had shifted Adela's inner schedule for going into molt. She would need extra food to strengthen her. Andreas would ask Nicholas for some eggs and cheese.

Later that day, when Andreas went outside to fetch wood, he heard a crunching sound. He looked down the path and saw a cheerful red-and-blue cart pulled by two sturdy mules, with their long ears twitching and steam blowing out of their nostrils. Nut-brown and solid, with a dusting of snow on their backs, they made Andreas think of sugared holiday cakes. A rider rode behind, leading another horse.

Richard and Gemma! Jubilant, Andreas ran to meet them. "I am so glad to see you!"

Richard nodded at Andreas. Gemma was completely wrapped in shawls. Only her dark eyes peered out. She did not bring the cart to a stop until it had reached the flat area in front of the house. Andreas scratched Paris between the ears, breathing in his comfortable scents of sweat and hay. The large mule rubbed his nose against his chest, almost knocking him over. Even Helen graciously allowed herself to be patted.

Gemma pulled down the shawls. Her face looked flushed. She laughed at him. "You look a lot better than the last time we saw you! How is the chicken?"

"The chicken?" Andreas sputtered and then started laughing in turn.

Richard dismounted and handed Andreas the reins. "Here, take care of the horses."

Andreas looked at Richard's back as he walked inside the house. "He hasn't gotten any more talkative, has he? Couldn't he at least have said hello?"

"Well, I wouldn't complain if I were you," Gemma said cheerfully. "He did come back up the mountain to get you, and believe me, it was quite a trip with the snow and sludge."

Andreas was not mollified. "He probably just wanted to get his gyrfalcon and the others."

"My, aren't we sensitive all of a sudden! Did you expect him to sit here and hold your hand while you sneezed?" Gemma laughed at him, taking the sting out of her words.

Andreas blushed. "I am really glad you are here!"

When Andreas came inside after settling the horses and mules, Richard smiled at him. "I am glad you are yourself again."

"When are we leaving?"

"Tomorrow. Get your stuff ready. We are going to be on the road at first light."

That night, Andreas ceded his pallet to Gemma. He and Richard slept on blankets on the floor near the fire. That is, Andreas tried to sleep while Richard and Nicholas talked until late in the night. They lowered their voices so Andreas could not make out what they were saying beyond snippets of words here and there. After a while, Andreas gave up and rolled himself into his blanket. He woke up a few times during the night; the men were still at the table, with a candle and a pitcher of ale in front of them, talking in a low murmur. Gemma snored softly under the sheepskin blanket. For a while, Andreas thought about the destination Richard wanted to reach by May. It was a castle in Apulia that Emperor Frederick II had built as a hunting lodge and mews. The name sounded glorious: Castel del Monte—Castle of the Mount.

They were outside at daybreak. It was a raw and chilly morning. Andreas shivered. He could see only the beginning of the road leading toward Bressanone. Everything else was hidden in fog.

He and Richard secured the birds in the cart. Andreas helped Gemma to hitch Helen and Paris to the wagon, while Richard led out the horses. Richard's horse, Trajan, a bay gelding, was a stumpy- looking, albeit reliable, workhorse. But he held his head with all the pride befitting a Roman emperor and could develop surprising speed when called upon. Andreas's chestnut mare had the more pedestrian name Hilde. The horses and the mules had grown thick coats over the winter months and looked well fed as if they had enjoyed a pleasant vacation.

Richard finished saddling Trajan. Giving the horse an affectionate pat on the rump, he went over to help Andreas with Hilde. A placid, kindly mare, she had one bad habit. She liked to inflate her belly; on route, she would blow out the air, and the saddle would slip. Now, Richard punched the mare's side while tightening the cinch. She shook her head, snorted, and then stood still, resigned to her fate. Richard went to his horse and mounted.

"Gemma, Andreas, we need to get going."

Gemma turned to Nicholas and spontaneously kissed him on his cheek. Then she hopped into the cart.

Standing next to his horse, Andreas was at a loss for words.

He had a lump in his throat.

Nicholas said, "Richard has access to the imperial post; you can write to me, care of the apothecary in Fortezza." He held out a small soft pouch. "This is for you."

Andreas pulled on the string. Inside was a piece of golden brown amber. Resting on its bed of green felt, it seemed to glow from within.

Nicholas said, "This comes from the Baltic Sea. Some people believe that it can heal many ills. Maybe it will help you one day."

"Thank you." Andreas stowed the pouch in his satchel. Then he had an idea. He pulled out the crushed bunch of the lavender, wrapped into a kerchief. Its fragrance was just as strong as when he had first hung it up to dry. "Mother used to dry lavender every year. I brought some with me from the hut in the woods. Here."

Nicholas took the small bundle and raised it to his face, breathing in the scent. He put his hand on Andreas's shoulder and smiled. "Go and finish what you set out to do."

Andreas nodded and mounted, although with some difficulty since Hilde picked that moment to step sideways. By the time they reached the first curve on the downward sloping road, the mist had already hidden Nicholas's house, nestled against the hills, with the Alps rising above it like sheltering hands. Andreas pulled up his horse and looked back. Then, sitting up straight, he followed Richard and Gemma on the road to Bressanone and the south.

PART V

MOVING SOUTH

How to Capture a Falcon

"Falcons may be secured in several ways. One may simply lift them out of the nest or catch them with various devices in the neighborhood of the eyrie as soon as they have left it. In the autumn they can also be caught when they are moving from one resort to another, fleeing from the cold. There is also a fourth scheme, one for capturing the birds in the regions where they pass the winter. A fifth plan (applicable to all birds) is to catch them as they return in the spring to the nest which they have deserted on account of the frosts of winter."

    - Frederick von Hohenstaufen, The Art of Falconry: Being the De Arte Venandi cum Avibus of Frederick II of Hohenstaufen

Chapter 17

THAT FIRST DAY ON THE ROAD, RICHARD CALLED FOR FREQUENT stops. Once, he checked a wheel on the cart. Another time, he slipped into the back of the cart and rummaged around for a while. Despite these breaks, Andreas was drained by midmorning when they stopped for a quick meal. His legs were sore, and he had to hold on to his horse for a moment after he dismounted.

"It is a mild winter." Richard said to Gemma and Andreas as they sat on a rock outcropping, with a couple of cypress trees providing shelter from the wind. "It will make our journey south a lot easier." He grabbed a branch and used it to draw a crude map of northern Italy into the dirt. "We are about here, near Bressanone." He pointed at a dot near a zigzag line, which, Andreas assumed, represented the Alps. "Our first task is to take the saker falcon to Verona. I have a buyer for him."

Chewing on a chunk of bread and cheese, Richard drew a line. "Here is the Brenner Pass, and here is Verona. We will travel to Verona via Bolzano and Trento. From Verona, we will pass through Rovigo and Ferrara. Our next major port of call is Bologna. You have to watch your step. Remember what I told you about the Guelphs and the Ghibellines?"

Andreas caught Gemma's eye. Clearly, the interminable history lectures had resumed.

Ignoring the byplay, Richard continued, reminding them of the different factions, shifting allegiances, and power plays of the day. Andreas had a hard time keeping it all straight in his head; meanwhile, Richard's stories made him think of a pack of dogs fighting over table scraps.

As they continued to travel south, Andreas forgot about these thoughts. The names of the towns rolled around in his head like musical notes; they evoked exotic worlds just beyond the horizon.

He was bewitched by the landscape, dotted with dark green cypress trees like beacons and gray-hued olive groves that held a promise of the coming spring. The red-clay roof tiles of the farms and village buildings looked cheerful and inviting. In German lands, sunlight was a precious commodity, and grapevines were squeezed onto narrow ledges on mountainsides along rivers, their location carefully calculated to ensure as much southern exposure as possible. Here, entire hills, gently sloping and fully exposed to seemingly unlimited sunlight, were planted with grape vines.

At inns, they were served huge platters filled with roasted vegetables that Andreas had never heard of. Andreas learned to dip his bread into a bowl filled with olive oil and pungent rosemary leaves. Used to a plain diet, he reveled in the crusty bread, dark olives, spicy fish, and wine in generous pitchers.

By now, all the birds had begun to molt. "Won't the buyer in Verona mind?" Andreas asked Richard worriedly.

Richard glanced at the falcons, woebegone like little old men with unkempt, thinning hair. "To be sure, they don't look like any king's ransom right now, but, no doubt, the saker falcon's new owner knows all about birds in molt." Nonetheless, he helped Andreas to make sure that their diet was augmented, sometimes adding extra meat, an egg, or cheese to their feed. Even though they were traveling quickly, they took the birds out in the mornings to keep them in shape.

"Nicholas told me that you have a knack for healing," Richard said as they rode toward Trento.

"He did?" Andreas did not know what to say. In the last few days, he had not thought much about his weeks with Nicholas. Riding along the sundrenched road, the hut in the mountains seemed part of a dream. It was not likely that he would be able to go to university to learn about medicine.

Anyway, first he had to take care of Adela. Maybe the emperor would offer him a post in the mews.

Richard glanced at him, but he did not say anything else.

Once they passed Bressanone, Richard used Italian more frequently. By now, Andreas understood most of it and found that he was able to respond with simple sentences, but he was envious of Gemma who was able to switch back and forth between

German and Italian without any difficulties. She helped him, often giving him the words for something or gently correcting his phrases.

By the time they reached Trento, Andreas was exhausted. He barely took in the grim looking gray facade of the fortress Castel del Buonconsiglio, the seat of the bishopric of Trento. He wished he could shut out Richard's voice.

"The bishops did a lot for the city. They developed the mining and wine-producing industries, encouraged trade, and fortified the city with new walls and towers. But when the bishopric became too powerful, Emperor Frederick handed the administration of its holdings over to Ezzelino da Romano."

The *clip-clop* of the horses' hooves echoed off the stone walls. Andreas thought of miners hammering at rocks in dark caves in the mountains.

"We will stay in Trento for the night. Tomorrow, we will travel on the Adige most of the way to Verona," Richard said, breaking into Andreas's thoughts.

"Really? We will go on a boat?" Andreas asked excitedly.

Richard smiled at him. "Well, a boat is stretching it. It's a river barge. It looks like a large tray without handles, but it does the job."

In the morning, before they headed for the river, Richard took Andreas to a building attached to the cathedral.

"Why are we going here?" Andreas asked.

Richard did not respond, just continued to the entrance. They walked along a narrow hallway. Buckets of refuse lined the wall. On a table, a pile of yellowed rags sat next to a pitcher of water and a stack of wooden bowls. Somewhere, someone was boiling cabbage. "What do you want?" They heard a woman's voice. When they turned around, they looked at a nun. She was pale, with dark shadows under her red-rimmed eyes and frown lines deeply etched into her face; but Andreas thought she was probably not much older than Gemma.

Richard pointed at Andreas. "I wanted to show my young assistant Trento's hospital."

"You are welcome to look around. We do the best we can." The nun hurried away.

In a large hall, about sixty people rested on pallets spread out in narrow rows along the walls. The air was rank with smells of sweat and illness. Most were oblivious to their presence. An old woman looked up as they passed by her pallet. She raised her bony hands as if pleading with them. One man coughed incessantly. Someone moaned, "Water, please, some water." Andreas could not see who it was.

When they returned to the hallway, they saw an older nun standing in front of an elegantly dressed man. His dark purple cloak was trimmed with fur and fastened at the shoulder with a jeweled brooch.

"Please, just take a look at him," she pleaded.

"Call me when you have a patient who can afford my fees." "It's just he is in such pain. All the sisters will pray for you."

"Hah! You better pray for them. These people are lucky to get all this care from you. I must go now. I am expected at the palace for an urgent consultation." The man swept past, never so much as glancing in their direction.

Richard went up to the nun and pressed something into her hand; then he gestured to Andreas that it was time to go.

"That's a hospital?" Andreas asked when they got outside. Gratefully, he sucked in the crisp air. "It's like a bad inn—worse. The infirmary in the abbey at Castle Kragenberg is better than this. And that man—he calls himself a physician? He is just a..."

Andreas sputtered; he couldn't think of a good word. "Why did you take me there?"

"I wanted you to see it," Richard said, but refused to say anything else.

Andreas was shocked. He thought of Nicholas's warm and welcoming hut with its array of fragrant herbs and the kettle of water on the fireplace, always ready to be used, and clean rags he used for binding up wounds. He thought of the dried lentils, small sacks of flour, and jars of olives that people brought in lieu of payment. Nicholas never asked whether anybody could pay for his services.

Silently, they walked back to the inn to get ready.

When they reached the river, they waited on the embankment until an unwieldy barge appeared, guided toward the dock by men with long poles. They had to lead the horses and the mules with the cart onto the dock and from there onto the barge. The horses were skittish, and Andreas had to put blindfolds on both. Richard helped Andreas to push the cart into the center and secure the wheels with wood blocks.

The Adige was swollen with the winter melt, and snow dotted the slopes on its banks. Once the barge had reached midstream, it moved swiftly downriver. Fascinated, Andreas watched barges being dragged upstream by teams of mules on the shoreline. They had the barge almost entirely to themselves; only a few other travelers sat on the low wooden benches. Two merchants, wrapped in their shawls, chatted quietly with each other. Andreas tried not to stare at a group of young men and women. Dressed in colorful tunics and leggings, their sleeves hung with tassels and little bells, they joked and laughed as if they owned the barge. One of the young men whiled away the time by juggling red, blue, and green balls. They had several flutes, a drum, and an instrument that looked like pipes sticking out of a large inflatable bladder.

"What is that?" Andreas whispered to Richard, pointing discreetly.

Richard glanced at the group. "Oh, that is a bagpipe. Wait till you hear it—a sound that is hard to describe, sort of funny and sad at the same time. I think this lot is going to be in Verona on Saint Valentine's Day."

One of the women smiled at Andreas. She wore a purple cap with yellow tassels over her short curly black hair, a bright blue tunic, longer than that of the men, and leggings that were butter yellow on one leg and dark purple on the other. Her face was painted, and large golden earrings bounced on her ruddy cheeks when she moved. Andreas watched, mesmerized by her red nails, as she broke off small pieces from a loaf of bread. She stuck them into her mouth in slow deliberate movements, glancing at Andreas through her long, dark lashes.

When they finally disembarked at a village near Verona, Andreas had to step over the entertainers' bags to get to the cart. As he passed the woman entertainer, she flicked his arm with her hand and chuckled. Her sweet and spicy scent made Andreas's nostrils prickle. Embarrassed, he turned to help Richard with the cart. Gemma glanced at him sideways, and he flushed. Then they got so busy with getting all their things off the boat that the moment passed.

Chapter 18

RICHARD'S CLIENT LIVED IN A CASTLE NOT FAR FROM THE RIVER. Surrounded by vineyards, it sat on a hill with a view of the river and Verona in the distance. The castle was enclosed by a high gray-brick wall. A late winter snow had dusted the turrets, bricks, and crevices with a light coat that glinted cheerfully in the sunlight. The gate opened onto a cobblestone courtyard framed by the imposing tower and the blocklike body of the castle.

After they had been announced, the count himself came out into the courtyard. Count Giacomo Razzi-Barini was short and stocky in build. He greeted Richard jovially, clapping him on the shoulders and giving him a swift embrace. "Riccardo, my friend! I am delighted to see you—and your increasingly lovely daughter." The count smiled at Gemma and then glanced at Andreas without comment. "I worried that you would not make it this year!"

"We ran into all sorts of delays on the road. You know how it is these days," Richard responded vaguely. Then he gestured toward the cart and asked, "Would you like Andreas to show you the saker falcon and put him through his paces?"

"Certainly, certainly, I would be delighted. Where do you want to do this?"

Richard looked around the large courtyard. "This will do for a short demonstration. Go ahead, Andreas."

Andreas nodded and hopped into the cart. He was nervous and fumbled with the equipment. Then he collected himself. This would be good practice. He was proud when he brought out the falcon. The bird was still in molt, and his feathers looked scruffy, but aside from that he was healthy and alert. Getting him to fly to the lure was by now something Andreas could handle with confidence. The falcon acquitted himself well.

The count beamed. "Well done! Riccardo, you brought me a

fine bird." The count called one of his servants over to take charge of the bird. Then he said, "Let's go inside and celebrate over a glass of wine. Of course, the *signorina* and your assistant are welcome to join us."

Gemma pleaded off. "Thank you kindly, but I would like to spend some time with my friend whom I have not seen for more than a year!"

A young woman, standing in a small group of people in the back of the courtyard and watching the demonstration, waved and beamed at Gemma.

"Ah, you remember Signorina Elena. Well, I am afraid she won't be with us much longer, since she got engaged. Go on. I will return your father soon enough." Bustling ahead, he led Richard and Andreas into the castle. "There is a nice fire going in my study. I will have some wine and cakes brought."

Andreas was amazed at the cordial welcome. He could not imagine Count Cuno asking Richard and his assistant to join him in his private quarters at Castle Kragenberg.

In the study, the count invited them to sit on large mahogany chairs with dark red brocade seats. Perched gingerly on the edge of his chair, Andreas looked around in bemusement. The elaborately carved mantelpiece on top of the fireplace showed the coat of arms of the count—a griffin crouching on the back of a lion. A pair of candelabras on top of the mantelpiece looked so heavy that Andreas was afraid they would come crashing down. The table next to him was covered with manuscripts.

A servant brought in a tray with goblets, a wine carafe, and a platter with an assortment of little cakes. Andreas watched Richard for clues on how to behave, marveling at his seemingly effortless ability to shift from his role as a humble trader to that of an honored, evidently welcome guest of an Italian count.

The count poured wine into the goblets, placed one next to Richard on the table, and with a kind smile handed one to Andreas.

Then he turned to Richard. "So, Riccardo, first to business. Tell me about the new falcon in my mews. Where does he come from?"

Richard picked up a goblet and tasted the wine. "You always have the finest wines, Conte, served in lovely rummers, no less!"

Richard held up the amber-colored glass so that it caught the light from the candles. It had a cylindrical base and odd protrusions on the thick stem.

The count looked pleased. "Well, you should know. Didn't you at one time include rummers in your trade goods? I imported these from a glassmaker in Worms. But do tell me about the falcon."

Richard leaned back comfortably, his dark hair and beard framed by the mahogany fretwork of the chair. "Ah, the saker falcon—I bought him from a merchant in Lübeck. He in turn got him from a hunter, who caught the falcon in the Great Steppe called the Puszta in Hungary. The saker was lifted out of its nest as a fledgling. The hunter is an experienced trapper and knows where to find falcons in the wild. Of course, he takes great risks in going so far east—the Mongols have overrun much of that area."

The count smiled. "That is a subtle way of saying that the considerable price you quoted is justified. Don't worry—you know me well enough. I don't like to haggle, especially not over such a fine and noble bird." He reached behind him and took a leather purse from a shelf. "Here, this has been ready for you for a while." He tossed it to Richard who caught it easily and put it away. "Now tell me, how was your journey from the cold north?"

Richard laughed. "You should get out more often. You might find the cold north is not as cold as you think."

Andreas listened as Richard talked. He was voluble in sharing colorful details of the journey, but less forthcoming when it came to talking about his other activities, never giving any hint of his role as an information-gathering agent working for the emperor.

Andreas's thoughts drifted. His eyes were drawn to the manuscripts. One tome was lavishly decorated with a centerpiece of ivory framed with jewels, next to it an open manuscript, revealing the vivid colors and gold leaf of the illumination. Luscious vines and blooming trees were the background for intriguing animals with curved horns, extra legs, and other peculiarities. They looked as if they had stepped out of one of the fables Brother Stefan had read to him. Then, his attention was pulled back to the room. Richard had stopped talking.

The count chuckled. "I always enjoy your stories. I am not much of a traveler, to be honest. Other than hunting, my preferred activity is to sit here and read." He poured Richard some more wine from the carafe. "I try not to get involved in the current tensions. It is not for nothing that our family shield shows a crouching griffin, biding its time." Then the count looked at Andreas. "And you, young man, what are you doing with my friend Riccardo?"

Andreas was surprised that the count would be interested in him. Before he could think of an answer, Richard interjected smoothly, "Andreas joined us this year. He has already proven himself most useful."

"Well, I watched you with the falcon and thought I might have just the spot for someone like you in my mews. How about it? Would you like to get off the road for a while?"

Andreas had just sipped from the goblet in his hand. The heady aroma of the red wine was unlike anything he was used to. He choked on it and started to cough. He was stunned by the offer. Every sensation—the feeling of wine in his belly, the scent of the cakes on the platter, the warmth from the fire, the manuscripts, and most of all the sympathetic kindly expression on the face of this rotund little man in front of him urged him to say yes.

And yet, his journey could not end here. Andreas shook his head to clear his thoughts. "Thank you. It is very kind of you." He glanced over at Richard, but Richard seemed absorbed by the color of the wine in his goblet. "Really, I am grateful, but I think I need to go on." He couldn't very well explain about Adela. Back on firmer ground, he added, "I owe Richard my services. I can't just leave him like that."

The count leaned back and smiled at Andreas. "I honor you for that attitude. All the more my offer stands. If in the future you would like to come back here, you would be welcome."

Chapter 19

AS THEY TRAVELED THROUGH THE PLAIN TOWARD VERONA, THEY could see the city straddling the river. To Andreas, riding in the lead for a while, the dense cluster of buildings looked like a balled fist, tightly curled to repel enemies from all sides. Standing up in his stirrups, he tried to get a better look. "What are all those tips that stick out above the rooftops?"

Richard mumbled something. Andreas looked back and started to laugh. Trajan trotted along looking half asleep. Richard held the cover of his satchel between his teeth, while he rummaged around in the bag with one hand, holding the reins loosely in the other. Then Richard dropped his hold on the satchel and said, "All is well. I was worried I had lost my permit. Anyway, those tips as you call them are towers, mostly of churches and palaces."

"What is the *palio* that the count talked about when we were leaving? Why did he suggest that we stay in Verona for that?"

"We are staying in Verona because I need to talk to some people. The count also gave me some references to people who might be interested in buying some of the silver I brought with me from a German silver mine. The palio just happens to be an added benefit. It is a race through the town that had been held for centuries. Actually, it is two races: one on foot and the other on horseback. But first, there is Saint Valentine's Day."

Gemma leaned out of her cart to get Richard's attention. "What happens on Saint Valentine's Day?" Andreas was glad that she had asked that question. He had been thinking about this ever since the encounter with the entertainers on the barge.

"Let me put it this way: There is not much that's saintly about this day in Verona," Richard said wryly. "It has a lot more to do with the ancient festival of Lupercalia, which originally was supposed to cleanse and purify the city and promote health and fertility. At least these days, the priests don't run around wearing goatskins, nor to my knowledge do they sacrifice any goats or dogs."

Setting a rapid pace, Richard led them up to the Porta Leoni, a city gate originally constructed by the Romans. All carriages and travelers entering or leaving Verona had to pass through this gate. They had to wait in line behind a motley crowd of people making their way into the city. Andreas saw the usual array of farmers bringing their wares to market, but also an assortment of entertainers and townspeople who looked as if they had already been celebrating all morning. A harassed-looking guard barely glanced at Richard's permit. Once through the gate, the noise level increased tenfold. Gemma, driving the cart, had to move slowly, her progress blocked by other travelers. Richard rode alongside, constantly on the lookout for people dashing into the road. Andreas had the rear guard. Hilde, normally not easily perturbed, bucked repeatedly, and it was by sheer luck alone that she did not kick anybody in her panic. Her neck and flanks were quickly marked with dark streaks of sweat flecked with foam. By the time they reached the inn that Richard had chosen, Andreas was worn out, his legs and arms still trembling from the tension.

The portly innkeeper stood in the courtyard chatting with a neighbor. When he saw them, he started to wave at them in emphatic denial.

"No, no!" he called out when Richard calmly dismounted. The innkeeper's voice rose higher. "Absolutely not! You can't stay here! We don't have room! Take your horses and your cart and go somewhere else! Don't you know what day it is?"

Unruffled, Richard walked up to him. "Ah, Signor Alberto, how quickly you forget your most loyal customers. Come, come, I am sure you can accommodate us."

The innkeeper's face lit up with a broad smile. "Oh, Master Riccardo, of course, how could I fail to recognize you? Of course, *you* are most welcome!"

The inn had a stable large enough to house their horses and mules and a covered area where the cart could be sheltered from the wind and occasional snow flurries. The innkeeper had become accommodating to the point of obsequiousness. It took no time at all to get a room. Richard arranged for one large enough for the three of them, so that Gemma would not be by herself in the women's area.

"This is no time to split up," Richard said quietly to Gemma and Andreas, once the innkeeper had left to make arrangements. A servant appeared to take them to their room; later she brought up some bread and ale as well as water in a jug.

When the servant had pulled the door shut behind her, Richard turned to Andreas and Gemma and said, "Please don't forget to watch your step. Take the innkeeper, for instance. Thanks to some hefty inducements, he is currently ready to support the emperor and hence willing to accommodate us. But you don't want to test his loyalty too much. Remember, Verona, more than any other place we have been in so far, is a beehive of conflicting interests, families at war with one another, diverse factions interested in supporting either the emperor or the pope for a gamut of reasons, and true loyalists on either side. Anyway, today is a day of celebration, which carries its own set of dangers. We will go out and have some fun, but you must promise me that neither of you will wander off alone."

Sobered by this warning, Gemma and Andreas followed Richard outside after their meal. It was snowing lightly. The noise level had increased and so had the crowds.

As they walked toward the center of Verona, Andreas did not know where to look first. Doorways were festooned with garlands. It was as if the entire city were in the grip of a fever. Veronese citizens, dressed in their finest gowns, crowded the streets; many wore colorful masks. Stalls selling food and wine at street corners were mobbed by hungry patrons.

It became clear that Richard knew the city well. Walking quickly, he led the way to a town square. He stopped in front of the Basilica of San Lorenzo. "This is one of my favorite buildings."

Andreas looked at Richard from the side and was intrigued to see that his normally saturnine face was flushed and animated. Then, trying to ignore the jugglers at the corner of the square, Andreas studied the church. The facade consisted of alternating tracks of brick and stone with two cylindrical towers replicating the same pattern. It exuded calmness and serenity.

Richard beamed proudly as if he had designed the building himself. Then he said, "Come, let's enjoy the day."

The next few hours passed in a whirlwind. At a market stall, Richard bought Gemma a woolen scarf woven in a pattern of dark red, gold, and black tones and with golden tassels. Andreas watched her wrap the scarf around her shoulders and smiled at her pleasure, but could not help feeling a pang. He envied her.

At that moment, Richard snatched up a dark blue cap, embroidered in gold along the edges. "What about this cap?" The woman named a sum, and Richard tossed her a few coins. Turning around, he placed it directly on Andreas's head. "There you go. Now, we are ready."

"Thank you!" Andreas flushed with pleasure and embarrassment. It was as if Richard had read his mind.

At another stall, they each got a stick with roasted meat and walked on. Jugglers, acrobats, musicians, and people with trained monkeys performed on church steps, in arcades, and in town squares. In one area, a stage had been set up and actors performed a play that had the audience laughing uproariously. Andreas could not make out the words, but the gestures of the burly men and women, tripping over buckets, waving brooms, and chasing one another all over the stage in pretended outrage left little doubt of their meaning.

Andreas marveled at the many languages he heard all around him, including German and others that he could not guess at.

"Wait here," Richard said suddenly. "I need to speak to someone." He ducked into a cobbler's shop, while Andreas and Gemma waited on the street, listening to a couple of bagpipe players. The sounds produced by the odd instruments reminded Andreas of Nicholas's flute. It was hauntingly beautiful, melancholic and full of yearning, an odd contrast to the atmosphere of revelry all around them.

Richard rejoined them, and they wandered on. In front of the town library, a man in tattered clothing, with hair sticking up in all directions and a beard that covered much of his face, shouted and shook his fists while crowds of people flowed past, oblivious to his ranting. "Repent, you sinners! Leave all this gluttony behind! Tomorrow, your doom will come! Repent before it is too late!" His voice was hoarse, and he looked ill and unkempt. His feet were bare.

Andreas was frightened and repelled.

Richard muttered, "He might have more of an audience once Lent has started. Today people are having too much fun."

Late that night, they finally headed back toward the inn. Andreas hummed a tune he remembered from the performance in front of the basilica. Gemma danced ahead of them. She had used some of the scent from the little flask that Richard had bought for her and floated along on waves of musk and patchouli.

"You look like you are herding cattle with all that jumping from side to side!" Richard laughed at her.

"I will have you know that I am performing a perfect rendition of the saltarello." Gemma twirled her scarf with enthusiasm and twisted and turned to the sounds of music reaching them from a distance.

They passed through a quiet town square. The only other people were a man and a woman. The man wore a brown hood that concealed his head and gave him a faintly monastic appearance. The portly woman was wrapped in a dark scarf that obscured her body. She carried a large basket. Her bulky shape reminded Andreas of Matilda—round, ruddy, energetic, and with an expression of exasperated affection when she caught him snitching bread from the kitchen.

At that moment, three horsemen cantered through the streets and onto the square. The couple glanced back and then started running.

Richard gripped his arm. "Be quiet," he hissed, and pulled Andreas and Gemma into a doorway. Andreas caught a glimpse of yellow and green bars on one of the shields as the soldiers thundered past. The man had already vanished around the corner; the woman stumbled with her basket in her desperate attempt to flee when the soldiers reached her.

The soldiers leaped off their horses and dragged the woman into a little alley. Andreas heard a sharp slap, followed by muffled thumps and moans. He tried to shake off Richard's tight hold but failed. Richard only relaxed his grip after the soldiers had remounted and ridden away. Finally, Andreas tore away from

Richard and ran across the square into the dark alley. The woman sat on the ground, with her back against the wall. She bled copiously from the temple and held her arms tightly wrapped around her chest. Her basket was upended with the contents strewn everywhere—colorful fabrics and woolen things lay on the slushy cobblestones.

Andreas crouched in front of the woman. "You are hurt. May we help you?"

The woman glared at him out of her one open eye. The other was partially closed, with a big bruise above it. She spat at him. "Get away from me!"

Taken aback, Andreas said, "I just want to help!"

"What do you think this is? A story of damsels in distress and brave knights? Mind you own business. Go play somewhere else."

Andreas hesitated.

The woman started to curse, showering him with a seemingly inexhaustible stream of invective.

"Let's go." Richard pulled Andreas up.

When they reached the next corner, Andreas felt queasy, suddenly regretting all the roast meat, pasties, and sweets he had eaten. He bent over and retched helplessly.

"That happened to me the first time I had hot mulled wine," Gemma said, patting him on the back.

At the inn, Richard asked a servant to bring a bowl and a pitcher with water up to their room. Andreas washed his face and hands and rinsed out his mouth to get rid of the foul taste. When he was done, Richard took the bowl from him and swiftly emptied it out of the window onto the bushes in the courtyard. Gemma sat on her pallet and began to knit. The sound of her needles clicking helped restore Andreas to a feeling of normalcy.

"That was awful. I wish we could have stopped those men."

Richard nodded, his expression grim. "There was nothing we could have done against those soldiers; besides, as you could see our help was not exactly welcomed."

"But why? What did she do?"

"Why did she get beaten? I have no idea. Perhaps she is an informer and got caught. Perhaps she stole something from the soldiers. Whatever it was, she is lucky to have gotten away with a beating."

Andreas studied the scuffed floorboards and something that looked like mice droppings. He still felt ill. "Whose soldiers were they?"

"Oh, Ezzelino da Romano; his coat of arms is easy to recognize."

"He is an ally of Emperor Frederick, isn't he? Does the emperor know about this sort of behavior?"

"You might be surprised if you read some of the articles in his legal code for Sicily, intended precisely to help defend women against violence and abuse. As to his alliance with Ezzelino, a struggle for a goal creates odd bedfellows and dirty linen."

"Everybody seems so opportunistic."

Richard said bluntly, but kindly, "What about you? Weren't you ready to use me as a way to get Adela away from Castle Kragenberg? Come to think of it, aren't you using Adela as a way to get yourself to a new life?"

Andreas picked on the straw that poked through the covering of his pallet. He had not thought of it in that way before.

"You and I are alike in many ways. Oswald told me a bit about you. Oh, you think Oswald didn't know what you were planning?"

Andreas stared at Richard. He remembered finding the old basket and the lure lying around so conveniently. Oswald had been helping Andreas all along. "Is he going to be punished for helping me steal Adela?"

"Don't worry; knowing Oswald, I am confident he covered his tracks well." Richard was silent for a moment. He scratched his beard, his expression thoughtful. "Look, I started out like you— without status or property or family. I hardly need to tell you that we live in a world where everyone, even your falcon, has a proper place. In some ways, that makes it all very easy. No choice, no questions, no doubts. But if you don't have such a place because of your birth or family misfortune or personal history, then it is more difficult. What choices would you have had if you had stayed in Castle Kragenberg?"

Andreas shrugged helplessly.

"You would most likely still be a kitchen boy, being chased around the table by Matilda for stealing bread. I certainly did not set out to be a trader. I wanted to be an architect. I tried to find a master builder to take me on as an apprentice, but I was unsuccessful. I did not know anyone with good connections to the powerful guild of builders and architects. On the other hand, if I had tried harder, I might well have succeeded. As it turns out, I am a pretty good trader, and my languages and my knowledge of the land come in handy in other respects. Besides, it gives me the opportunity to work for something I believe in." With a self-deprecating, mocking smile he added, "Of course, in the meantime, I always hope for another Count Razzi-Barini who would offer me a sinecure, my own little place in the sun. But is has not happened yet. Incidentally, what made you turn down the count's offer?"

"I don't know." Andreas spoke slowly. "I suppose it would have been Matilda all over—safe, comfortable, and totally confining."

"Well, that's one way of looking at it." Richard stood up. "It's time to get some sleep. We have to be on the road tomorrow."

Gemma looked up from her knitting. "Tomorrow already? I thought we would stay until the *palio*. I was looking forward to that!"

Richard was blowing out the candles. "I got a message today. I have to get to Ferrara as soon as possible."

The last candle went out with a hiss. Andreas heard Richard sit down on his pallet and pull off his shoes. When Andreas closed his eyes, it seemed as if the room and everything in it was turning around like a huge wheel. Carefully, he sat up again; the dizziness and nausea lessened. To distract himself, he thought about the woman in the alley. He should have done something and not let Richard pull him away. Still, the woman had made it quite clear that she did not want him to interfere. Andreas tossed and turned all night. His dreams were populated by monkeys dancing to the sound of bagpipes, voluptuous, scented women chuckling softly as they brushed past him in the crowded streets, and an itinerant preacher with foul breath who cursed and spat at him.

Chapter 20

THE NEXT FEW DAYS, RICHARD SET SUCH A PUNISHING PACE THAT Andreas had no energy left to think about the events in Verona. The only respite came when he took out the birds for their exercise. Richard, by this point, had consigned that task over to Andreas almost entirely. When alone with the birds, Andreas talked to Adela. Sometimes he was convinced she knew and reacted to his voice. Then, looking at her unwinking black eyes, he felt like a lost traveler standing outside a cast iron door that would never open.

They used a ferryboat to cross the river Po. They stayed at an inn on the outskirts of Ferrara. It was not easy to find adequate stabling for the horses, mules, and falcons as well as accommodation for themselves in crowded city centers. Their room had a damp smell, and the pallets looked flat.

"We might as well sleep directly on the floor," Gemma said dispiritedly.

Andreas tentatively sat down on one of the pallets. Compared to his pallet at Castle Kragenberg, this one was not so bad.

Gemma sniffed at the bread that a servant had brought up on a tray together with a pitcher of ale and some beakers. "Moldy again, Father."

Richard had just pitched the contents of his beaker out of the window after having taken a careful sip of the ale. He nodded. "I am not surprised. Don't worry, we will find better fare elsewhere. Gemma, would you see to it that the mules get new shoes?"

Gemma looked resigned. "It is better than staying in this hovel. I'll go look for a blacksmith. I'll see you later."

"And I need a bath," Richard said briskly. Then, looking at Andreas speculatively, he went on, "And so do you."

Andreas scowled. "Why? I scrubbed myself just a few days ago." He thought of the bucket with scummy water he had used to rinse his hands.

"Come on, a proper bath won't hurt you." Setting a rapid pace, Richard led Andreas through the town gates into the San Pietro district.

Andreas had become accustomed to the way in which, in Italy, buildings were built directly up to the street front, with narrow gates leading to spacious interior courtyards. Still, he was surprised when Richard stopped at a gate he had not even noticed and with the assurance of someone who had been there many times walked past the fountain in the courtyard to a doorway. They each received a towel and a brush with a long wooden handle from the attendant and walked through another door into an antechamber.

The walls were lined with hooks and benches. "You can strip and leave your clothes here." Richard was already pulling off his tunic.

"This is a bath?" Andreas asked in amazement.

"Yes, you can thank the Romans for that. The Ferrarans are very proud of it and keep repairing it." Richard finished hanging up his clothes. "Are you coming?"

Andreas gaped at Richard's muscled torso with a crisscrossing of scars. "Oh yes, of course." Hurriedly, he stripped and trotted after Richard. They entered a room that was so steamy that at first Andreas could not see much at all. A large square basin was edged with polished gray-and-white marble slabs and filled with steaming water. People sat on the edges and in the basin. Three women were engaged in an intense conversation, oblivious to their colorful tunics billowing up in the water around them. Most of the men had stripped. Some rested on pallets. One lay on his belly; an attendant rubbed oil onto his back and then proceeded to give him a massage. Another played softly on a lute. A man with a basket walked up and down, offering snacks and flasks of wine. A gray-haired man sat on a stool, with a servant behind him carefully trimming his hair. Two men played cards, using a board as a floating table; they took occasional sips from flasks standing on the edge of the pool.

This was not Castle Kragenberg. When he was younger, Matilda had sometimes grabbed him and dunked him into a wooden vat, scrubbed him vigorously, and then poured cold water over him to rinse him off.

Bemused, Andreas slipped into the water. It was hot but not

uncomfortable. He closed his eyes. Sounds of talk and laughter echoed in the high-vaulted stone chamber, blending into a soothing backdrop to his thoughts. He rubbed the scar on his hand. It had healed well, but he could still feel the puckered skin.

Suddenly, water rushed into his nose, and he came up sputtering. He had fallen asleep. Rubbing the water from his eyes, he realized that Richard was engaged in an intense conversation with two men, one burly in build with a shock of silvery gray hair and the other slender and dark, next to him in the water.

"When is this supposed to take place?" That was Richard. "At the end of the month." The gray-haired man coughed. "Does Enzio know?" Richard asked.

"No, it is safer for all that he knows nothing of this until the last minute. That's where the boy comes in." The man spoke softly, but Andreas heard him as if he had shouted. Goose bumps sprang up all over his back and arms.

"I am not convinced that this is a good idea. I want to think it over. I'll send a message before we get to Bologna," Richard said.

The man frowned. "It's not that easy to find someone young enough to look innocent and yet discreet and intelligent enough for the task. Let us know soon."

"What about me? What am I supposed to do?" Andreas interjected. He pushed himself out of the water and sat on the edge of the basin.

Richard raised an eyebrow and responded mildly, "Ah, you woke up. Nothing is decided yet. I'll explain at the inn. Let's go back before we get waterlogged."

Coming outside, water still dripping from his head, Andreas shivered in the late winter chill. They walked back to the inn in silence.

In their room, Richard sat cross-legged on the floor in their room and began to polish his saddle. Andreas stared. He had never seen Richard do any of the day-to-day work other than handling the horses and the mules when they got recalcitrant.

"Surprised? You have not seen me do lots of things."

Andreas sat down on his pallet. "This is about getting King Enzio out of Bologna, isn't it?"

"Yes," Richard said curtly. "But nothing is decided yet."

"What can I do? Why haven't they tried before? What's the plan?"

"One question at a time. First of all, they have tried before, but it is difficult. Several people have already been caught and lost their lives. I don't know the details yet, but the plan is to smuggle Enzio out at the end of the month. And you, well, you heard me, I am not sure I want you to be involved."

"Why not?" Andreas asked.

Richard looked away. Then he said, "For one, freeing Enzio might well result in more battles and more deaths. He would be a rallying point for both supporters and haters of the Stauffer dynasty."

Andreas was stunned. "But you spent all this time showing me what Emperor Frederick has been trying to accomplish, such as support of trade and laws for the proper administration of justice and universities. Enzio could help to support all that."

Richard was silent. He looked tired and strained.

Watching Richard's closed face, Andreas was puzzled. It was as if they had traded places. In Verona, he had been shocked by the things that happened directly under the eyes of the emperor; now it was Richard who seemed to want to back off from everything.

The door opened and Gemma stepped into the room. She carried a tray. "The horses got new shoes, but that was the grumpiest blacksmith I have ever met. Look, I got some edible stuff from the kitchen. They couldn't very well refuse me once they realized that I had seen their stores. I guess they save the moldy bread for guests who don't know any better." Proudly, she placed her tray on the table. There was a loaf of crusty bread, cheese, a bowl of olives, and a carafe of red wine.

"Excellent timing, my dear." Richard got up and poured wine into three cups, mixing some water into each. He handed one to Gemma and one to Andreas.

With fastidious fingers, Gemma fished an olive out of the bowl and put it in her mouth. "These are good olives. You should try some."

Neither Richard nor Andreas paid any attention. After a silence, Richard said wearily, "Maybe I am getting too old for this. Look, I believed and still believe in the benefits a strong empire could provide—not least of those peace and stability. That's why I began to serve as one of many eyes and ears working for the emperor." Richard stretched out his long legs. "But you are just starting out. It occurred to me that we have no right to drag you into this."

Andreas began to get angry. "Isn't that my choice to make?"
"Of course," Richard said heavily. "I just want to make sure you

think it through. Anyway, we don't know enough details yet. There is still some time to find someone else suitable for this job —we won't get to Bologna before late March."

Over the next days, there was no further discussion about the plan to free Enzio. Richard made an evident attempt to talk to Andreas and Gemma about unrelated matters, often joking and amusing them with his witty descriptions.

As they moved south, Gemma began to shed more of her shawls. The horses seemed to enjoy the sunshine, and even the mules needed less prodding.

"Do you know one of the nicknames of Bologna? They call it the city of the three *t's: torri, tortellini, e tette*—literally 'towers, tortellini, and tits'—begging your pardon, Gemma." Richard twisted in his saddle to observe the effect of his words. His beard had not been trimmed for a few days, and he looked scruffy, but his eyes smiled.

Gemma laughed at him. "Why those three?" she asked.

"Well, *torri* for all the many powerful families, each with their own tower reaching into the sky. *Tortellini* for the delightful little tidbits made of eggs and flour and stuffed with meat or cheese—I will get you some. Usually, they are prepared only for the Christmas feast, but I think I can convince an innkeeper I know to make an exception. The food in Bologna is fabulous. Hence the other name, *La Grassa*, or 'the Fat One.' And *tette*— well for all the beautiful women of this city!" Richard airily sketched a womanly shape.

Andreas and Gemma laughed. But Richard was not finished. "They also call it *la Dotta*, 'the Learned One.' And indeed there is a wonderful university, one of the oldest and most renowned in all of Europe. If you were going to study law, you would come here. You can also study medicine and philosophy."

Andreas imagined studying medicine at the University of Bologna. Then he shook his head. He might as well bat his head against the wall. He could not afford to do something like that.

Gemma made a face. "Forget philosophy. Tell us more about the food!"

"Typical! I offer to talk about philosophy, and all you can think of is food!" Richard said in an affronted tone. "But I must admit—the food is spectacular. Wait till you get to eat mortadella!" Richard looked positively elated at the thought.

"Oh, Father, can we please get some in the village where we are staying tonight?" Gemma pleaded.

"Now that is an excellent idea."

"What's mortadella?" Andreas asked, intrigued by their delight. "Oh, mortadella, the queen of food! The most supreme of all sausages! You are in for a treat!" Richard's eyes gleamed.

"The Romans were the first to prepare this sausage and knew a good thing when they found it. It goes really well with an omelet. Of course, the Bolognese claim that they alone know the secret ingredients. They definitely include peppercorns, coriander, and anise. I am not sure of the others."

The roads on route to Bologna were dusty and uneven, with many areas washed out by the winter melts. They were constantly on the lookout for rocks and boulders that would trip up the horses or damage the wheels of cart. Yet, Richard rode in a relaxed, loose- limbed fashion with an easy-guiding hand on the reins. Glancing at his dark face from the side, Andreas thought that Richard had paid quite a price for his convictions. Life on the road was hard, with dangers and discomforts awaiting him everywhere.

A few days before they were due to reach Bologna, they spent the night in a barn in exchange for some cotton fabric that Richard had purchased in Verona. After Andreas had finished taking care of the birds and helping Gemma feed the horses and mules, he walked around in the half-light of the early evening. The days had gotten noticeably longer. Andreas bent down and picked up a pebble. He lifted his arm and threw it at a cypress tree down the road. He heard the little thud as it hit the tree.

Andreas turned and went back to the barn. Gemma and Richard had already set up the pallets. Richard sat on his, sorting through his satchel. Gemma glanced up and gave Andreas a cheerful nod, never stopping her knitting.

He stood in front of Richard and said, "Look, I know it's a risk. I've thought about everything you've said. But I really want to do this. Let me help in Bologna."

PART VI

KING ENZIO

On the Proper Care of a Falcon in Captivity

"When a suitable location for the care of falcons has been found, an artificial nest must be built of materials like those of the wild eyrie. This place should be open on three sides (to the north, east, and west breezes) and exposed to the morning and evening sunshine."

- Frederick von Hohenstaufen, *The Art of Falconry: Being the De Arte Venandi cum Avibus of Frederick II of Hohenstaufen*

Chapter 21

"WHAT IS THAT MAN DOING?" ANDREAS POINTED AT A FIGURE on the side of the road.

Richard was taciturn and abstracted, riding silently with his head bent. Now he glanced up to see where Andreas was pointing. The man, if it was a man, wore a dark green gown, his face hidden by a hood. Andreas heard the *click-clack* of the clapper suspended from the man's belt as he lurched along the road with awkward jerking movements.

"That is a leper; keep your distance," Richard responded abruptly. He turned to Gemma. "Give him plenty of room as you take the cart past."

"Why? He looks harmless." Andreas was perplexed. Vaguely, he recalled people at Castle Kragenberg talk about leper colonies, but he had not been interested enough to find out more.

"Let's keep going; we have a lot of ground to cover today."

Andreas realized he would not get anything out of Richard about this. When they passed the man, Andreas tried to peek at his face, but the hood was in the way. He looked back a few times, curious and frightened. Gradually, the figure shrank into the distance, the lurching motions mocked by the sounds of the clapper, incessant and merciless—a dissonant lament.

They stopped for a rest in a village near Bologna. It was chilly, but the midday sunlight was pleasant. Richard walked off without a word. Andreas watered the horses and mules, while Gemma rooted around in their supplies to see what they had to eat.

Having finished with the horses, Andreas walked to the back of the cart.

Gemma turned around. Her face was streaked with tears.

"Gemma? Why are you crying?" Andreas was shocked. He had never seen Gemma lose her composure.

Gemma used her sleeve to wipe her face. "Because of the

leper on the road today."

"What about him?"

"Have you heard about leprosy?" "Yes. Well, not really."

"It is a horrible illness. Nobody knows what causes it. It starts with spots on your skin. Eventually, it eats away parts of the body. It is like rotting alive. When people get it, they are chased off and made to wear those gowns and clappers, so people know when a leper is coming." Gemma glanced around to see whether Richard was nearby. Then she went on, speaking softly. "My mother got leprosy several years after I was born. The villagers drove her away, forcing her to live in a leper colony, even though she was pregnant at the time. She died there."

"Oh, Gemma, that's awful!"

Gemma shook her head impatiently. "It was a long time ago. I just get upset whenever we see someone with leprosy. My father tried to visit my mother a few times before she died, bringing her food and clothes, but she refused to see him. She died giving birth to a baby boy, who died right after. My father had me stay with my mother's sister for a while. My aunt made me sleep in a corner in the barn; she was afraid of catching leprosy from me. Some people say that lepers are holy people because of their suffering and that their prayers are powerful. I don't know how that does them any good."

The sound of steps alerted them to Richard's return. "Are you two ready? I want to reach the inn in Bologna before nightfall." Richard spoke briskly. Gemma and Andreas packed up quickly. Neither of them had eaten anything. Andreas was glad to have something to do, and he avoided looking at Richard.

The road was busy with travelers. Riding alongside the cart, Andreas thought about leprosy. Maybe one could get it from breathing the air. Surely, they had not been close enough to the poor man. He wished Nicholas had told him about this. He wondered whether healers visited the leper colonies. But he did not dare to ask Richard. The *clip-clop* of the horses' hooves kept Andreas thinking of the sound of the clapper.

They reached Bologna in the late afternoon. The red roofs of the city, accentuated by many spiky towers, glowed in the sunlight. A construction project was in progress along the outer wall of the city. Richard pointed it out to Andreas and Gemma. "This is one of the largest cities in Europe and growing rapidly. So they need to expand and build new city walls."

They passed through the Porta Saragozza, one of the gates leading into the city. Andreas was impressed by the broad road beyond the gate. "Is this the main road?" he called out to Richard.

Richard nodded. "You like the Via Emilia? The Romans built it, like many other streets in Bologna. It is pretty easy to find your way around here; everything is laid out like a grid— nice and clear."

The inn turned out to be run-down, but with enough stabling and room for the cart. Richard, helping Andreas and Gemma with the animals, was annoyed. "This place has fallen apart since I was here last. When I think of all the money I paid the innkeeper over the years, I could weep. The stable is a pigsty, and I am afraid the rooms are not much better. But it's not as if we have all that much choice right now."

Once again, Richard had decided on a single room rather than sending Gemma off to the women's common room. Their room was small and grimy, with a few moldy cheese rinds from a previous tenant, and mouse droppings from the permanent ones. The bedding smelled musty. Gemma insisted on carefully checking everything for bedbugs, and she borrowed a broom from one of the servants. When she had finished, she held up her shoes. "Father, I am going to look for a cobbler. Don't your shoes need new soles as well?"

"Good idea." Richard handed her his shoes and some coins.

Shortly after she had left, there was a knock on the door.

Richard opened it and waved two men inside. "Umberto, I am glad to see you."

Andreas recognized the small dark-haired man from the bath in Ferrara. The other one, tall and gaunt, looked at Andreas appraisingly.

The small man clasped Richard's hand and embraced him. Then he nodded toward his companion. "Taddeo, a cousin of mine. He will bring the horses for getting Enzio out of Bologna."

A carafe with wine and another one with water stood on the

table. Richard poured wine for all of them, adding water to each cup. "Well, gentlemen, it is cramped in here, but at least we don't need to shout. What exactly is the plan?"

Taddeo spoke first. "It all hinges on timing. Someone has volunteered to be a stand-in to help dupe the guards for a night. They are changed all the time, and a new set of guards started just yesterday. The only ones in regular contact with Enzio are his personal servants, and they also are changed often, because the city elders found that he became too friendly with them. Anyway, they don't come more than once a day. That gives us some time to implement our plan."

Umberto coughed and said, "Now, Andreas, Richard told us that you agreed to help. We need you to go into the palace and bring a message to Enzio to prepare him. Are you still willing to do this?"

Andreas nodded. His throat was dry.

"Could you elaborate on the plan? Won't Andreas be searched when he enters the palace?" Richard spoke sharply.

"Well, yes, of course. Everybody is." Umberto paused to drink some wine. "Don't get me wrong. Enzio's prison is a bit of a gilded cage. Bologna wants to keep its royal prisoner in style. He is in the Palatium Novum. That's a new palace built in 1245 with all the trimmings in many of its apartments, for all that it also has the standard dungeons and prison cells. Enzio's apartment is above the dungeons. During the day, he can move about in the wing of the palace where he is being kept, and he is allowed visitors. But Andreas definitely cannot carry a written message."

Taddeo took over. "Tomorrow morning, we meet at the Shower of Gold tavern near the prison. You deliver the message. A troupe of entertainers together with the stand-in arrives in the early afternoon. The stand-in wears distinctive clothing and a large floppy hat with tassels and carries a lute. At that point, Enzio and the stand-in change clothes, while the entertainers dance and play music. After a suitable interval, the entertainers leave with Enzio. He carries the lute and plays along with the others, while lurching about as if drunk. The stand-in stays behind, rolled up on Enzio's bed. The guards will see someone who looks just like Enzio fast asleep, and they will leave him alone. In the morning, he will claim that he was drunk and cannot remember what happened."

Andreas bit his lip. He wanted to say something, but Richard preempted him. "This stand-in—who is he? Why is he willing to risk his own freedom or even his own life in this venture?"

"Ah, I am glad you are asking." Umberto spoke with evident enthusiasm. "This man is perfect for the part. We would be hard-pressed to find someone else as suitable. Giovanni is a distant scion of the Galluzzi, one of the leading Guelph families in Bologna. Even better, he has a reputation as being silly— nobody would ever associate him with something like this. He is a minor poet with a penchant for singing romantic songs with atrocious melodies underneath the window of whoever happens to be his mistress of the week . . . or day. More to the point, he looks the part—tall, well built like King Enzio, and with a shock of reddish-blond hair. His face doesn't look anything like the king's, but once Giovanni is bedded down, seemingly fast asleep as if in a drunken stupor, nobody will be able to tell the difference."

Richard studied him quizzically. "And no doubt he is aware of his good fortune in participating in this charade?"

"Oh yes, you see, that is the beauty of it. He is a secret admirer of Emperor Frederick. With touching frankness, he told us nobody would suspect him of having been a willing party to this deception, since nobody ever takes him seriously anyway—not to mention having the family name for protection. He never had the courage to break with his family openly; he is too indolent and enjoys the easy life. But he is intelligent and clever underneath all that flimflam of courtly love and bad poetry."

"How do you propose to get Enzio out of the city?" Richard asked.

Taddeo responded, "He is going to ride out in plain view. Once the entertainers together with Enzio reach the street, they are supposed to walk a few blocks to where I will be waiting with horses and mules. When they arrive at the gate, all looking equally seedy and wasted from too much partying, along with crowds of other revelers, nobody will bother to take a second look."

Finally, Andreas got up his courage to speak. "How long

should I stay with King Enzio? Do I leave right after delivering the message?"

"Good question." The dark-haired man smiled at Andreas approvingly. "That will depend on how busy the guards are. If they let you out quickly, that's fine. Otherwise, you can go out with the entertainers."

That made sense to Andreas. "What will be my excuse for going into the prison? Why would the guards let me in to see Enzio?" "You will be carrying a dish of food as a present from a lady admirer of Enzio's. Enzio receives such gifts frequently, so the guards are used to it. In fact, they love to joke about it. The food sounds pretty good to me—a lamb stew with *pignoli* nuts and raisins." Taddeo beamed enthusiastically, as if he expected this marvelous dish to materialize right in front of him.

"I see what you mean by a gilded cage," Richard said with a smile. "Incidentally, I heard a rumor to the effect that at night the guards place Enzio in a cage that is suspended from the ceiling. Is that true? It seems that would lead to a much earlier discovery of his escape."

The two men looked astounded and almost affronted. Umberto said, "Where did you hear that? It's ridiculous."

Richard got up. "Good. I hear all sorts of things on the road. It does not hurt to check. Speaking of lamb stew with *pignoli* nuts, I want to take Gemma and Andreas to get some dinner—I promised Andreas some of your wonderful Bolognese food. Will you join us?"

The two men shook their heads. The tall one said, "Thank you, but we have to meet with someone. We will see you tomorrow morning."

Chapter 22

IT WAS A MILD EVENING. IT SEEMED AS IF HALF OF BOLOGNA'S citizens were outside, talking and laughing. Andreas was glad of the distraction; whenever he thought about the next day, he was filled with apprehension.

They walked across the Piazza Maggiore and looked at the palace where Enzio was imprisoned. In the half-light of the early evening, its clean lines and simple gray-pinkish sandstone facade gave the building a soft and inviting character. It was hard to think of this elegant edifice as containing prison cells and dungeons. The roof was lined with whimsical looking sickle-shaped merlons, the stone structures sticking out all along the parapet, reminding Andreas of bishops' hats sitting side by side. In one area of the building, an arcade opened onto a courtyard, giving the building an almost churchlike aspect.

Richard led them past other palaces and pointed out the university.

Andreas gaped at the large building. "That is a place just for studying? It's huge!"

"Impressive, isn't it? Some of the finest scholars in all of Europe work there."

Wherever they went on the city streets, they saw narrow tall towers dotting the landscape—grim vertical fortresses. "What are these towers supposed to do?" Andreas asked.

"I am not entirely sure. I suppose they are like symbols. Each major family tries to build a tower like that. It is almost a sport— to see which one can build the tallest."

Their meal included mortadella, the sausage Richard had waxed poetic about, and tortellini—little ring-shaped pieces of dough—stuffed with cheese and boiled in water. Their shape made Andreas think of the tightly curled tail of a piglet.

Richard held up one of the tortellini. "You know what they say about these?"

Gemma shouted excitedly, "Oh, Father, let me tell it!" Richard grinned at her and nodded.

Gemma stood up and made a serious face as if about to declaim Homer's *Odyssey*. "One dark and stormy night, a long time ago, when the seas were wine-dark and the gods were still walking among humans..." Gemma paused and pretended to pluck strings on a lyre before she continued. "The lovely goddess Venus and stern, powerful Jupiter arrived at a tavern in Bologna. They were exhausted from having participated in a battle between the cities of Modena and Bologna. After much food and drink"— Gemma looked inquiringly at her audience— "should I list the food and drink?"

Andreas and Richard both laughed, shaking their heads.

With a reproving expression on her face, Gemma continued, "Well, it was very good food, but you are evidently too simple to appreciate it. Anyway, replete and tired, they shared a room. The innkeeper was bursting with curiosity, never having hosted Venus or Jupiter before. He usually had to make do with the lesser gods, who tended to walk out without paying their bills. So, brushing his hands on his flour-covered apron, he tiptoed after them. Once they had entered their room and pulled the door shut behind them, the innkeeper put his eye to the keyhole. And do you know what he saw?" Gemma looked at Richard and Andreas expectantly, waving them on encouragingly as if they were a Greek chorus.

Andreas, mesmerized by her performance, said, "What?" "Nothing! That is, all he could see was Venus's belly button,

nice and round and curled up on itself. He stared and stared, and then he clutched his head as if struck by lightning. Dazed and muttering to himself, he turned around and accidentally knocked over the thunderbolt, which Jupiter had placed next to the door. Without paying attention to the resulting crash and the sparks, the innkeeper rushed to the kitchen, moaning in his excitement, and began to create tortellini in the image of . . ." Gemma paused for dramatic effect and then concluded triumphantly, "Venus's belly button!" She sat down, beaming, while Richard and Andreas banged their wooden tankards on the table in appreciation.

Later, Andreas asked Richard about Enzio. "Did you ever meet him?"

"Yes, I met him once after a battle and found him to be friendly and easygoing. I think you will like him. He loves falcons, so you have something in common. You know that he has a German mother?"

Andreas shook his head. "Who was she?"

"A woman by the name of Adelaide. Emperor Frederick did not marry her. At court, these things don't matter so much."

"Does he speak German?"

"Yes, well enough, though Italian is really his language by now. People say he even writes poetry in Italian."

"It is amazing that the emperor cannot force Bologna to let Enzio go."

Richard frowned at Andreas. "Haven't you been listening over the last year? These city-states are very powerful, in some ways more powerful than the emperor. Bologna would never let him go."

Andreas cradled his tankard; he tried to imagine being locked up in prison for the rest of his life, never to be able to ride across the fields or to fly a falcon.

"Why did they decide to do it this week?" Gemma asked to break the silence.

A servant placed a large platter of bread and cheese on the table and replenished the carafe with red wine. Richard cut a piece of cheese and ate it with an expression of delight. Chewing thoughtfully, he mumbled, "Well, the feast of the Annunciation was on March twentyfifth." He poked at the cheese.

"Father, that's not an answer!" Gemma chided. She and Andreas looked at Richard expectantly.

"It's perfect for our venture. Conveniently for our purpose, the ancient Roman festival of Hilaria with its celebration of spring coincides with the feast of the Annunciation. It goes on for several days, and it gets pretty wild. Many people wear disguises and masks, and it seems that every year people come up with new tricks to play on each other. The guards will be nice and mellow after so much feasting and drinking." Richard sipped some wine, studying Andreas over the rim of his goblet.

"Why don't we use masks tomorrow?"

"Think about it. If Enzio wears a mask when walking out, it might provoke a guard to check what's underneath the mask and look too closely at his face. If he doesn't wear a mask and is surrounded by a rowdy group of drunken entertainers and revelers, the guards are less likely to give him a second glance— especially when they remember someone with the same build and same clothes walking in. It's called hiding someone in plain sight. People see what they want to see."

All of a sudden, it felt chilly in the little tavern, and the headiness of the evening had evaporated. Gemma rubbed her arms and pulled the shawl closer around her shoulders.

Richard stood up. "Let's get back."

Andreas did not sleep much that night. He tossed and turned, unable to shake images of rusty chains and rats scurrying across damp stone floors in windowless dungeons. To distract himself, he tried to picture himself riding across the hills in Apulia with King Enzio on a royal charger. Surely, Enzio would help him with Adela. He might even offer him a position in his army.

In the morning, Andreas checked on the horses and mules as well as the birds. The stable was dark and smelly; nobody had taken out the soiled straw and horse dung in days. He grabbed a pitchfork and cleared the area where the mules and horses were standing. When he was satisfied, he threw down some clean straw. The birds were quiet. Andreas refilled their water bowls and fed them just the right amount to last until nighttime. He was pleased that they waited calmly for him rather than screeching and flapping their wings. Oswald had always told him that the way to wean birds off this bad habit was to have the same person feed them at the same time and in a quiet space. Andreas worried about Adela. She had been cooped up for a while now and probably would start fretting soon. He could not wait to fly her in the hills of Apulia.

Richard was in the courtyard, waiting for him. Suddenly, Andreas was flooded with embarrassment at the thought of meeting a king, with his hands still grimy from mucking out the stalls. He tried to brush off bits of straw stuck on his hose. "Richard, I don't have anything else to wear."

Richard glanced at Andreas's stained and worn tunic. "You are not exactly invited to a banquet at court. You look just right for the role of a messenger boy bringing a gift from Signora Lucia. But you better give me your purse. You'll be searched."

Hastily, Andreas untied the leather purse he always wore around his waist and handed it to Richard. He had just a few coins and the amber stone from Nicholas in it.

"I'll keep it safe. Come on, we have to meet Umberto and Taddeo."

Richard walked along with his usual loose, long-limbed stride as if he did not have a care in the world.

Andreas, trying to match his stride and attempting to look relaxed, asked, "Who is Signora Lucia?"

"She is a lovely woman with a gift for cooking who has been enamored of King Enzio for some time—from the distance, mind you, always hoping to be invited to meet him. She is a *contadina*, a peasant woman—albeit a wealthy one who can afford to send all sorts of gifts to Enzio. She has a big heart. When she was approached by the conspirators about a dish as camouflage for the messenger, she readily agreed. She did so, even though she knows quite well she will never see Enzio at all if he should be so lucky as to make his escape. Kings and peasant women rarely mix."

"There they are." Andreas pointed to Umberto and Taddeo standing in front of a tavern in a pool of sunlight. The two men nodded in greeting, and together they entered the tavern. Andreas blinked as his eyes adjusted to the dark room. There was nobody else inside.

Taddeo bolted the door. Umberto lit a candle and placed it on a table. Then he grabbed a few beakers and a carafe of wine from the tavern's counter. "Sit down. Relax—we bribed the owner to let us have the room to ourselves this morning. Here, have some wine!"

Richard shook his head. "Thank you, maybe later," he said tersely.

"Here is Signora Lucia's offering." Taddeo reached under the table and brought up a large basket. "She did herself proud. This should keep the guards entertained!" With a flourish, he lifted the linen cloth covering the contents. Scents of fresh bread, savory spices, and cheese rose from it. Andreas could see two clay dishes with covers and several flasks of wine.

"Gentlemen, I am sure this is all perfectly delightful, but can we go over the plan once more?" Richard spoke in his customary dry and sardonic tone.

Umberto nodded. "Don't worry. We've got it all worked out."

Together Umberto and Taddeo walked Andreas through the plan. On a wax tablet, they drew a little street map, pointing out the palace and the way back to the inn. They made him repeat what he needed to tell King Enzio.

"Andreas, do you have any questions?" Richard asked.

Andreas shook his head. He kept his heels pressed firmly to the ground to keep his legs from shaking.

Umberto folded up the map. "It is time for you to go."

Andreas stood up, relieved that the waiting was over, and grabbed the basket.

Richard went outside with Andreas. He said quietly, "I will be waiting for you at the inn." He put his hand on Andreas's shoulder and looked as if he was going to say something else. Then he dropped his hand, and Andreas turned and began to walk.

Chapter 23

ANDREAS COULD FEEL RICHARD'S GAZE FOLLOWING HIM AS HE moved down the street. The basket was heavy and awkward to carry, and the walk to the end of the street seemed to take forever. He went around the corner and along the next street directly onto the Piazza Maggiore.

Andreas stood still for a few moments, trying to gather his courage. The great square was filled with people, many already in costumes. Pigeons flew around, landing here and there on the flagstones of the square and looking for food. Guards flanked the large gate in front of the palace, two on each side. Andreas could see their helmets glinting in the sunlight. They wore dark red leggings underneath their chest armor, short swords hung off their belts, and each held a long pike. The two guards on the left stood up straight, looking into the crowd without expressions on their faces. The other two chatted, leaning on their pikes like old men on their shovels.

The basket seemed to have gotten heavier. Andreas forced himself to move slowly so as to appear relaxed as he walked across the square and sauntered up to the guards on the right side of the gate. Mustering a cheeky tone, he said, "Good morning. I have a delivery for King Enzio."

"Really? And what might that be?" One guard, with a splendid mustache and a ruddy face, turned toward Andreas with a bored expression.

"Signora Lucia prepared a meal for him." Andreas held up the basket.

The guard raised his eyebrows. "Signora Lucia! She is truly devoted! At this rate, King Enzio is going to blow up to look like a dumpling soon."

The other guard leaned over and lifted the linen cloth to peer at the contents. "Let's see what's in here." He lifted the cover of the clay dish. Andreas could see meat swimming in a rich broth. The guard smacked his lips appreciatively. "Maybe you should just leave that with us, young man."

Andreas pulled the basket back protectively. "I can't do that. Signora Lucia would whip me if I did not deliver it in person and report back on how he liked it."

"I am sure she would. You probably deserve it. But go on. I don't have time for this." The guard twirled his mustache and then shouted, "Claudio, open the gate! There is a delivery for our royal guest."

Hinges squealed as the heavy gate was pulled back. The gatekeeper looked as if he had spent the last decade in a windowless dungeon—pale, with thinning hair, and a gray tunic that hung loosely on his bony frame. He glanced at Andreas with weary eyes. "Put the basket on the table."

Andreas watched as the gatekeeper fastidiously shook out the linen cloth and poked around in the contents. He picked out a little packet, sniffed it, and put it on the table without comment.

"Empty your purse."

Andreas patted his tunic. "I don't have one," he said apologetically.

"Stand still then." The gatekeeper ran his hands up and down Andreas's back and sides, lifted up the tunic, and poked an impersonal hand into his hose. Andreas could smell the gatekeeper's bad breath, and nausea welled up in his stomach. The gatekeeper stepped back. "Well, come along. I don't have all day."

Andreas followed the man into a dark stairwell, lit by only a few torches on each level. As they made their way up the stone steps, Andreas glanced around furtively, taking in heavy cast iron doors and small barred openings in the wall on every level. Sounds of groaning reverberated in the stairwell. He heard a woman singing. The voice was filled with wild exuberance; it turned to shrill laughter, followed by gurgling and sobbing. Andreas changed his grip on the basket; his hands were clammy, and his tunic was damp with sweat.

Finally, they reached the fifth level. A guard stood in front of the door. He eyed the basket with an expression of envy and said, "What a life! Prisoners get fancy baskets full of delicacies, and we have to make do with barley and water!" Then he shrugged and opened the door. He pointed down a long hallway. "Just keep going all the way through those doors at the end."

The city rulers had dedicated an entire floor to their royal prisoner. Enzio's apartments stretched across several large rooms. Andreas slowly walked along the hallway through a set of wooden double doors into a spacious room with a vaulted ceiling and windows overlooking the courtyard. Amazed, he took in the stacks of books on a large table in the center. Velvet-covered chairs surrounded the table. Another door was at the opposite end of the room. Andreas waited for a moment and then knocked.

"Come in." It was not a deep voice, but strong and well modulated.

Andreas pulled the door open and entered. A man with a shock of reddish-blond hair and a broad back sat at a table facing the window. The sunlight was filtered by iron bars across the window, the only reminder that this was in truth a prison. The room was comfortably outfitted with carpets and velvet curtains. A chessboard was set up on another table, with a carafe of wine and silver goblets next to it. Andreas could see a recorder and a lute on a shelf. The man raised his head from his work and turned around. There were shadows under his eyes.

Andreas bowed. "I am bringing a basket from Signora Lucia and also a message from friends."

Enzio looked at Andreas courteously, but with an expression of polite disinterest. "Well?"

"There is a plan to help you escape, my lord."

Enzio abruptly pushed away what he had been working on and stood up. He was a tall man. He walked over to the window and looked out. He moved like a soldier, with straight- backed discipline. But, to Andreas, it seemed that he had no energy, like a bird after molting. After a moment, he spoke softly. "Come here. Tell me."

Andreas put down his basket and approached the king hesitantly. Andreas could well imagine this man commanding an entire army. But his face was pale, as if all the color had leached out of it, and oddly slack. It was hard to believe he was just thirty years old. For a moment, Andreas thought of the youthful rider on the tapestry in Castle Kragenberg.

"It will be today." Andreas explained the plan.

Enzio expressed amazement when Andreas told him about the stand-in. "How odd! I have heard about Giovanni. In fact, one of my friends joked about him. And here he is willing to take a risk to help me. I guess I will eventually have to do him the courtesy of reading his poetry though I hear it is perfectly dreadful." He walked to his desk and sat down. "And you? You are German, aren't you?"

"Yes. My name is Andreas."

"Well, Andreas, make yourself comfortable."

Andreas hesitated. When Taddeo had told him he might have to stay with the king until the troupe of entertainers came, Andreas had thought he would sit in a corner and wait.

"Come to think of it, we might as well explore this lovely basket." Enzio seemed almost lighthearted now, as if playing a game.

"Won't a guard come and check on me or make me leave?" Andreas asked shyly.

"Oh no, my keepers don't mind your staying here. I'm the one who has to stay. That's why the plan is quite clever. The guards will be distracted because of the festival. It won't raise any eyebrows at all to have a rowdy bunch of entertainers come trooping in and trooping out a bit later and even rowdier. Now let's see what the good Signora Lucia sent us."

Andreas put the basket on the table and opened it. "The guard downstairs took one of the packets for himself. I think it was cheese." Enzio laughed. "Poor fellow! I don't blame him. Don't worry about it. I have been getting rather tired of Gorgonzola." He gingerly poked at the contents of the basket and pulled out two wine flasks, waving them in the air triumphantly. "Now if he had taken these, I would have been unhappy. Here it is—the conveyor of sweet dreams and the deceptive mantle of innocence for our own Giovanni!" Andreas helped to take things out of the basket. It was a feast.

In addition to the stew and the wine, Signora Lucia had sent dried olives, cheese, a chunk of mortadella, and bread. A heavy, sticky cake made with figs, walnuts, and honey was tucked at the bottom.

"You better take this cake back with you. It hurts my teeth." Enzio rubbed his hand over his jaw. "The barber tells me that he will have to pull one of them when he comes next. I don't look forward to that."

Andreas looked at Enzio more closely and realized that one side of his face was swollen. Getting a tooth pulled had to hurt. Then he remembered something Nicholas had said. "If you could get some sage and rosemary and make a tea, you could rinse with that. Warm water with salt would also help with the soreness."

"Really?" Enzio's blue eyes narrowed as he studied Andreas. "You surprise me. Sit, sit. You can't stand there all day. Here, have some wine. Now tell me how a nice young man from Germany ended up in my prison in Bologna."

Gingerly, Andreas sat down, perching on the edge of the chair. He watched Enzio put some stew on a platter and hand it to him.

Enzio looked at him speculatively. "I think you are just about the age that I was when I first joined my father at court. It does not seem all that long ago." Enzio waved the bread knife at Andreas. "Some bread and cheese?"

Andreas nodded, still uncomfortable. But Enzio kept prodding him with questions, and Andreas found himself telling Enzio about his life—working as a kitchen boy, running away with Adela, and traveling with Richard and Gemma.

"I wish I could see this famous Adela. I hope you will find a home for her." Enzio paused, looking thoughtful and as if he wanted to say something else. Then he shook his head. "It's not for me to advise you."

Andreas nodded. Briefly, he wondered what Enzio was not saying. Perhaps Enzio thought that his plan of going to the emperor would not work, but he had heard this already from Richard and Nicholas, so he shrugged it off. Meanwhile, he was puzzled by Enzio's attitude. It was as if Enzio were outside of time and space. He was not apparently thinking about the escape plan or the notion of being a free man again after a year in captivity. Instead, evidently grateful to have an audience, he talked to Andreas as if to his younger self.

"Like you, I love falcons. My father believes that the study of falcons and their nature is equivalent to a study of life and its dynamics. I am not that ambitious. For me, it is just for the love of it. Nothing equals the experience of watching a falcon roam across the sky in unconstrained majesty and then gracefully return to your fist like an honored guest. Here, let me show you. I have been whiling away the time with writing and drawing."

Enzio rummaged in the pile of papers on his desk and pulled out several sheets covered with drawings. There were falcons on perches, falcons in flight, falcons stooping over prey, sketches of wings, and profiles of falcons with their powerful beaks.

"My royal father paid dearly for his love of falconry—perhaps you have heard of the Battle of Parma."

"What happened?"

Enzio told the sad story. In the winter months from 1247 to 1248, the city of Parma was being gradually forced to its knees. During the siege, the emperor had constructed a wooden city outside the city walls where he kept his treasure and his entire menagerie, from which he did not want to be parted. One day in February, the emperor went on one of his hunting expeditions. He came back to find that, during his absence, the camp had been assaulted and taken, his menagerie destroyed, and his treasure gone. In the ensuing battle, the imperial army was badly defeated.

"But he could not have known the attack would come at that time!" Andreas surprised himself by daring to speak.

"Perhaps not, but he should have known, and he should not have left the camp. A good leader would have known." Enzio's expression was severe and with a hint of bitterness. Then he shrugged and held up the serving spoon invitingly. "Here, have some more of this stew. You are my guest in a manner of speaking."

Andreas watched Enzio ladle a generous helping of food onto his plate. "Thank you."

Enzio pushed away his own plate. Restlessly, his fingers broke up a piece of bread. "I think my father simply tried to escape from his burdens for a day. His happiest times are when he is surrounded by the scholars and writers that he attracts to his court and where the only thing that really matters is the life of the mind."

Andreas found the thought of the emperor trying to escape his burdens an uncomfortable one. He did not know what to say.

Enzio turned his face to the window. It was as if he had forgotten Andreas. Speaking in a low tone, he said, "Sometimes I think I am well out of it. It is not easy to be a Hohenstaufen these days. We are banned by the pope. My father, my brothers, indeed everyone bearing the name of Hohenstaufen and everyone loyal to us—we are all hunted and hated. My father has many hopes for the kind of world he wants to create. But it seems to come down to brutal slaughter on open fields, everyone fighting for a slice of power. Meanwhile, here I sit, warm and cozy, fed with olives and wine, and with entertainment brought to me—anything the heart desires. And yet there is no open sky, no wide field to canter across, no falcons in flight. I am trapped in a silken web, and my friends avoid talking to me about the outside world for fear of hurting me."

Enzio began searching among the papers on his desk and pulled out several sheets. "I have begun to write poetry. At least there might be something left after I am gone."

Bemused, Andreas listened as Enzio read to him. He did not understand everything, but he loved the musical tenor and flow of the language. There was a poem about a battle; the sounds of clanging swords, gasping horses, and breaking bones reached Andreas through a filter of rhythm and rhymes. Repeatedly the word *libertà*—freedom—rang out like the stroke of a sword upon a shield. There was a poem about a falcon in flight, and another about love. One was called "The Night."

No, not asleep
With all the world around him Sunken into torpor
He alone is awake; his gaze
Travels across silken seas, gentled by the wind.
The unyielding sky has imprisoned the stars,
And the land has vanished.
Free and serene, emptied of longing,

He is lost in the sweetness of dawn.
Eya! shouts fill the void. Eya!
Once more, the clamor of the palace! And the bell tolls.

Enzio fell silent.

Andreas glanced at the bars on the window. The wall of the building across the courtyard seemed close enough to touch. Suddenly, Andreas was brought back to the reality of the situation. "My lord, do you need to make any preparations?"

Enzio started as if waking from a dream. Then he stood up. He took some papers from the table, folded them, and stuck them inside his hose. "There is nothing else that I will take. It would just make me more conspicuous."

He walked to the window and back, casting his eyes around in the room as if he could not remember where anything was.

Andreas gathered the dishes and towels and placed them back in the basket. He watched Enzio pace back and forth. It made him think of the mindless weaving of a falcon on a perch when stressed or ill. Then he had an idea. Hesitantly, he said, "My lord, would you like to play chess?"

Enzio stopped abruptly. "Now there is a capital idea. Do you play?"

Andreas said, "Not very well. Someone taught me recently." "Good enough. Let's play."

They played silently. Enzio was outwardly calm, but all his easygoing manner of earlier had evaporated, and he often seemed to cock an ear toward the hallway.

To Andreas's amazement, he found that he could hold his own against Enzio. At first, he was tense and nervous. He worried about the planned escape, and his stomach hurt. But after a while, he decided to concentrate on the game. He took one after another of Enzio's figures, methodically lining up one of the bishops, a rook, two knights, and several of the pawns in front of him.

"Check," Andreas said, feeling proud of himself.

A clanging sound down the hallway startled him. Voices were faintly audible through the thick wooden doors.

Enzio tipped his king over. "You play well." He looked Andreas squarely in the eye. "Thank you for the game. I am glad they sent you today."

Chapter 24

LAUGHTER AND SINGING GREW LOUDER. ANDREAS HASTILY STOOD up, knocking over the basket next to the table. The remnants of their meal spilled onto the floor, and he started to cram things back into the basket. Enzio leaned back in his chair; holding a goblet of wine in his hand, he watched the door with an expression of polite disinterest as if receiving courtiers for a particularly boring presentation.

The doorway was filled with entertainers, several with bells sewn onto the sleeves of their tunics and carrying musical instruments including a fiddle, a flute, and cymbals, two jugglers, and a young woman who looked like a dancer. Andreas looked for the stand-in; he was perplexed not to find anyone who would be a likely candidate. The last one to enter was a short, squat person with a full beard and a whimsical long red cap with a tassel dangling off the tip. He staggered inside in the wake of the others, holding on to the doorframe, as if he could barely stay upright. Then he closed the door and straightened up, now appearing completely sober. He glanced at Andreas and then stepped up to Enzio, bowed briefly, and talked to him in a low tone.

Enzio grew still. For an instant, an odd expression flickered across his features. Andreas stared at him; it was as if the king was relieved. Then it was gone, leaving behind a face drawn and shocked.

The entertainers fell silent and glanced at the short man. He gestured to them to continue. "Go on for a bit. Make it look real."

Andreas snuck up to the short man and whispered, "What is happening?"

The man spoke softly out of the corner of his mouth. "It's off. The stand-in is dead. He got stabbed last night in a tavern. There was nobody to take his place. You are coming back out with us."

Andreas thought there was nothing quite as joyless as

watching jugglers and fools clown around to the sound of music in a world gone gray with hopelessness. He could not bear to look at Enzio, sitting at his desk as if frozen.

The grating musical performance seemed to go on forever. Finally, the performers stopped and Enzio stood up. He straightened his back and held himself proudly. He turned to Andreas. "You were most gracious to spend the day with me." He pulled the bundle of papers out of his hose. "Would you take this to my father?"

Andreas hesitated, unsure whether to say anything, but after a quick glance at Enzio's face, he just nodded and hid the papers under his tunic.

Enzio smiled at him; for a moment, he looked young and mischievous. "Perhaps one day you will finish telling me the story of Adela! Good luck!"

The leader made a sign to his troupe. They all bowed and walked out. The leader approached Enzio and said, "We will try again, my lord."

Enzio nodded courteously, waving his hands as if dismissing a supplicant at the conclusion of a successful audience. "My door is always open to you!"

Like a group of boisterous children returning from an outing, they made their way down the hallway. The guard looked at them with indifference. They pushed past him noisily. Their laughter echoed in the chilly stairwell as if in mockery of the sounds of groaning and shouting from the cells.

Andreas stumbled on the steps. The leader reached out a hand to steady him. The grim expression on the man's face stood out starkly against the face paint and the bright red cap with its cheerful tassels. He leaned closer and whispered. "My name is Roberto. We'll stay with you until it is safe. Then you have to make your way back to the inn."

Andreas nodded. At the bottom of the stairs, the cavernous-looking gatekeeper slouched on a chair in a dark alcove next to the door. He got up and pulled back the heavy cast iron bolts on the door.

The din and roar of an entire city in a convulsion of festivities was deafening. Crowds of revelers milled about in the glow of late afternoon sunlight.

"The basket! I forgot the basket. Won't Signora Lucia be angry?" Dismayed, Andreas stopped walking.

Roberto smirked. "By no means! This will vastly improve her chances with the king."

"What do you mean?"

"Oh, she is simply drooling at the thought of cooking more meals for Enzio, always hoping to be invited to visit him in person. Don't worry; she'll get her basket back in no time. Let's move."

The crowd pushed past their small group like a river swirling around floating logs. Someone jostled Andreas's arm. It was a slender man with an ivory mask and a long tunic, a nobleman going out for a night on the town. For an instant, Andreas looked straight into dark eyes, like polished beads in the pale mask, and then he heard a chuckle. It sounded like a woman. Before he had time to assimilate this, he was pushed forward, and he struggled to keep from falling onto the pavement, sticky with food and spilled wine. The mix of odors from the crowd—sweat, unwashed bodies, and musky perfumes— made him want to gag. Then he became aware that the air turned increasingly acrid.

"Roberto, what's that smell?"

Roberto spoke brusquely. "It's a fire. Come on!"

Andreas had a hard time keeping up with Roberto. He tried to focus on the red cap, swinging from side to side ahead of him. The smell of fire grew stronger. The cacophony of raucous festivity gave way to the sounds of people screaming and yelling and horses galloping along the street. Andreas gasped and coughed; sweat ran down his face.

The troupe had reached the corner of a street leading away from the Piazza Maggiore. Roberto pointed at a gate in the wall halfway down the street. It creaked softly as he pulled it open, and they entered a courtyard. A stone faun, with his gray surface deeply pitted, presided over the murky water of the basin, one moss-covered foot in the water and the other raised provocatively. He held a bunch of grapes in his hand and leered at them out of his stony toothless mouth. The entertainers looked at one another, out of breath and frightened. Gesturing to them to stay silent, Roberto kept his eyes pressed to the gap between the gate and its frame.

The noise intensified as people ran past their sanctuary. The sound of horses cantering over the cobblestones reverberated in the little courtyard. Standing close to Roberto, Andreas could hear dull hollow thuds followed by screams. Eventually, it got quiet.

Looking left and right, they exited from the courtyard. Along the street and around the corner, people sat on the pavement or leaned against a building wall, some moaning in pain, others just looking dazed. Smoke hung in the air like a haze.

"Do you think the fire is close?" Andreas asked Roberto as they hurried along.

"Oh no, we are not in any danger. It is at the edge of this district," Roberto said distractedly. He kept glancing around, and Andreas thought momentarily of a falcon looking for a prey.

"How do you know that?"

"I should know. I set the fire myself." "You did? Why?" Andreas was shocked.

"It was supposed to burn just a few old oak barrels; I guess it went out of control. It was planned as a distraction for getting Enzio out of the city. I had not envisioned our getting nearly squashed by the crowds and beaten by the city guards as a result."

Andreas was silent, appalled by the enormous consequences of an effort to rescue one man. He trotted along, his head bent and feeling tired to the core.

Then Roberto cuffed him. "Hey, this is no time to fall asleep. Can you find your way from here? It's quiet in the streets now, and you shouldn't have any trouble getting back."

Andreas looked up. He recognized the street and knew in which direction he would have to walk. He nodded. "Thank you."

"It was nothing. Stay well." Roberto turned, and he and his troupe disappeared around the corner.

When Andreas walked through the gate, he found Richard in the courtyard, brushing Trajan with methodical circular strokes. The horse looked sleepy and content. Andreas inexplicably felt tears well up when he saw this calm scene.

Richard took one look at Andreas's face and put down the brush. He whistled, and a boy came out of the stable. "Here,

Benito, finish up and take Trajan back inside." Then he put an arm around Andreas's shoulders and steered him into the inn.

Sitting with a mug full of hot spiced wine in his hand, Andreas told Richard and Gemma about everything that happened that day.

Gemma listened with fascination to Andreas's description of the library and the room where they had spent most of the day. She looked thoughtful. Then she said, "As prisons go, it does not seem too bad. At least he can do some of the things he likes and even have visitors. Besides, he is warm and well fed."

"But he is not free!" Andreas said.

Gemma nodded. "True, but then who is? Think about it." Richard looked grim. "This was the third attempt. It's a shame.

It sounded so promising."

"Will they try again?" Andres asked.

"Certainly, but they have to wait for another good opportunity."

Lying on his pallet in the dark room, Andreas thought of Enzio in his gilded cage with pity and grief. He remembered snatches of a poem that Enzio had read to him, speaking so softly that Andreas had to strain to hear it.

Fear grabs me by the entrails
that I might never again see the glory of the sun
forgotten here and as if buried long ago.

PART VII

CASTLE ON A HILL

On the Proper Aims and Qualifications of the True Falconer

"The falconer must not be one who belittles his art and dislikes the labor involved in his calling. He must be diligent and persevering, so much so that as old age approaches he will still pursue the sport out of pure love of it. For, as the cultivation of an art is long and new methods are constantly introduced, a man should never desist in his efforts but persist in its practice while he lives, so that he may bring the art itself nearer to perfection. He must possess marked sagacity; for though he may, through the teachings of experts, become familiar with all the requirements involved in the whole art of falconry, he will still have to use all his natural ingenuity in devising means of meeting emergencies."

- Frederick von Hohenstaufen, *The Art of Falconry, being the De Arte Venandi Cum Avibus of Frederick II of Hohenstaufen*

Chapter 25

"WITHOUT A DOUBT, THE ANCIENT ROMANS HAVE BEEN VASTLY useful in some respects," Richard said to Gemma and Andreas. They sat at a table in a common room of an inn south of Bologna, with a pitcher of ale and a platter with bread and cheese in front of them. "Thanks to their industry, we will be able to travel mostly on decent roads as we journey south to Apulia."

Using twigs and pinecones from the basket of kindling, Richard laid out the coastlines and the principal cities and regions of central and southern Italy on the table's surface. "We are here, in Emilia Romagna, and here is Apulia. We will follow the Roman road south and east to Ravenna." With his finger he traced the route on the map of twigs. "From there, we can travel all the way down the coast to Apulia. Castel del Monte is not far from the coast." Richard set a pinecone on the spot.

Gemma bent forward to take a better look. Her curly dark hair fell out of her cap. "Why are we not going along here and from there down to Apulia?" She drew her finger down the middle of the map, in a direct line from Bologna to the south.

Richard smiled at her. "Sorry, bad map. Bologna is closer to the east." He shifted the pinecone. "Going along the coast is the best route. There is also another consideration."

Andreas studied the map. "I know! You want to stay away from Rome, right?"

Richard nodded. "That's right. Rome, the pope, and the plague of Guelphs. We are better off traveling the other way." He stood up, swept up the twigs from the table, and tossed them into the hearth. "Let's get going."

Over the next few weeks, Richard set an easy pace. It was spring, and the hills were bathed in a silvery green mist of budding olive trees. Richard and Andreas began getting up earlier and earlier to take the birds out. Gemma sang a lot, and often Richard joined in. Gemma tried to teach some of her songs to Andreas, but he declined. He could not carry a tune and preferred to listen to the two voices, one high and clear and the other a full baritone. For a while, he stopped worrying about what would happen once they reached Castel del Monte. His daydreaming gave way to exhilaration when they approached the coast. He could feel the closeness of the sea in the air, breezy with a bracing tang, and the quality of the light, ever more intense and glowing.

In the evenings, Richard spent a lot of time writing. When he noticed Andreas watching him, he said, "I am working on a report for the emperor. We covered a lot of ground over the last six months."

Occasionally, Andreas caught a look of wistfulness on Gemma's face. "Are you all right?" he asked her one evening, when he saw that she had dropped her knitting on her lap and simply sat, lost in thought. She looked at him with a pained smile. "I am just homesick."

"But you don't have a home! You are always on the road." "Exactly. I finally want to arrive somewhere."

Andreas was silent. Traveling with Richard and Gemma had given him more sense of home than he had ever felt before.

In Ravenna, one of Richard's clients purchased the lanner falcon. Andreas was relieved that Adela still had the merlin and the gyrfalcon to keep her company on the last portion of the journey.

Before heading back to the inn, Richard took Gemma and Andreas to see a mausoleum in the center of the city.

"You won't get a chance to see something like this very often," he said implacably, when they asked why he dragged them to look at the tombs of people who had died more than seven hundred years earlier. "They say that Galla Placidia, the daughter of Emperor Theodosius, had this built as a mausoleum for her and her family, but nobody knows for sure." Inside the cross-shaped interior, Gemma and Andreas were silent as they looked around. Illuminated by a gentle light entering through alabaster window panels, the central dome was a vast dark blue space filled with countless golden moons and stars. Andreas was awed by the enormous labor and the exquisite precision with which thousands of tiny mosaic tiles had been fitted together.

It got warmer by the day. To Andreas's intense delight, a few times they stayed on the beach at night. Gemma slept inside the cart, and the two men were rolled up in blankets on the sandy ground, sheltered from the wind by the sun-bleached cliffs. Andreas did not sleep much; he looked up at the sky and listened to the waves. In the mornings, they took the birds flying on the heights, soaring in the clear air high above the rocky landscape.

Steadily, they traveled south. Andreas was mesmerized by the changing landscape. When they reached Apulia, it was as if they entered another country. The mountain chains that gave the regions further north such a stern and harsh appearance softened into undulating hills along the coastline, whitewashed rock formations reaching out into an intensely blue sea, and vast broad plains further inland. Vegetation was sparse. The land was stripped bare, leaving nothing but light and space and low- growing bushes with a spicy fragrance released at sundown.

Andreas saw more wild hunting birds and other birds than he had seen in a long time.

"This is a good area for birds; many rest here before flying further north for the summer; falcons even breed here—they like the shoreline with its cliffs and the wide open spaces inland," Richard told Andreas.

Richard made use of the longer days by stretching the distance they traveled every day. There were not many villages in this sparsely populated region. Riding along in Richard's wake and squinting in the sunlight, Andreas closed his eyes. He was comfortable on Hilde's sturdy back. Dipped into relaxing darkness, he listened to the *clip-clop* of the hooves and Gemma singing softly in her cart. All of a sudden, he heard Richard call out. Andreas opened his eyes. Richard had stopped and was pointing at something in the distance.

Andreas pulled up his horse next to Richard. "What is it?" "There she is. The crown of Apulia."

In the distance, Andreas could see a gently rising area like a vast, raised island mountain, topped by a glowing white structure that did indeed look like a crown in the sunlight. "That's the castle?"

"That's the castle." Richard affirmed. "We are half a day's ride away. We will stop overnight in the next village." He picked up the reins, pointing at a wooded area further along the road. "If I am not mistaken, there is a stream just beyond that wood and a village. I stayed there the first time I was here."

The dusty road curved slightly downward. Richard swiveled in his saddle to watch Gemma guide the mules carefully along the slope. Andreas rode along in the back, mesmerized by the white structure in the distance.

Suddenly, Andreas heard a muffled curse followed by a crash and a scream of agony. He could see Trajan rolling in a cloud of dust. Richard had disappeared. Andreas jumped off Hilde and ran around the cart to see what had happened. A section of the road had crumbled, taking horse and rider along with it into the ditch; Richard was on his back, one leg caught underneath the horse. Then Trajan was up; he climbed out of the ditch, snorted, and shook himself vigorously. When Andreas reached Richard, he had fainted.

Gemma had already stopped the cart. She jumped down and rushed to her father with her skirts flying.

Andreas raised his head and shouted, "Put blocks under the wheels!"

Gemma turned around quickly, but fortunately the cart had not moved, and the mules stood there placidly swishing their tails. She grabbed the blocks from their usual storage place and secured the cart. By the time she got back, Andreas had already dragged Richard out of the ditch and placed him on level ground. Andreas took off his tunic and rolled it up as a pillow. Then he looked at Richard's leg. It looked bad. When Trajan fell, rolling over Richard on the way down, one of the horse's hooves must have hit it. The hose was ripped, the lower part of the leg lay at a funny angle, part of the bone was exposed, and a deep cut ran almost halfway across the leg.

Gemma knelt down. She touched Richard's face, and Andreas could see her hand tremble. For some reason he could not identify, this calmed him down.

"Gemma, listen to me. You need to go for help. I'll stay with Richard and guard him. Take Hilde and go to the village. Bring back some people."

Gemma hesitated. "I don't want to leave him." "You must. We can't take care of him here. Go!"

Gemma nodded. She got up and turned to Hilde, standing placidly next to the cart. Gemma pulled up her skirt, bunching it up between her legs so she looked as if she were wearing wide baggy pants. She mounted awkwardly. She kicked Hilde, and the horse started to move.

For a moment, Andreas watched the cloud of dust that enveloped rider and horse. Then he turned back to Richard. The sun was directly overhead, and it was hot. Andreas looked around. An umbrella pine on the other side of the road provided shade. He left Richard and went over to Trajan, who was nuzzling some scrubby growth near the ditch with his left hind leg lifted. When Andreas led the horse over to the tree, he saw to his relief that Trajan put weight on the leg and limped only slightly. Andreas tied him to a branch.

Then Andreas climbed into the cart. He gathered several items and went back to Richard. He dropped his stash and returned to the cart one more time. Richard sometimes used a wooden board as a ramp for rolling heavy objects in and out of the cart. That would come in handy. It was a bit too long and broad for what Andreas had in mind, but it would have to do for now.

Richard was still unconscious. Andreas thought that was just as well. He knelt next to him and placed the board directly alongside the leg. Then, he carefully pushed his hands under the leg and lifted it onto the board. He tried not to touch the area where the bone was exposed. He ripped rags into thin strips and proceeded to tie the leg to the board in several spots along the leg, above the knee, around the ankle, and right under the knee, just not near the wound. He took a blanket and gently eased it underneath Richard's body. Richard looked pale, but he was breathing. Andreas braced himself, grabbed the corners of the blanket, and pulled. Fortunately, the ground was even, and the blanket slid along despite Richard's weight. Andreas tugged on the blanket until Richard was in the shade.

Richard groaned. He opened his eyes. "What happened?"

"The road crumbled under you. Trajan slipped into the

ditch and fell on your leg. It's broken."

Richard said something inaudible. Then he tried to sit up. "Where is Gemma?"

"Don't move. Gemma went to get help. She took Hilde." "Oh good." He closed his eyes. "What about Trajan?"

"He is favoring his right hind leg a bit, but he is putting weight on it. I think he'll be fine." Andreas held out a small flask that Richard always kept in the cart. "Here, take a sip."

Richard peered at the flask and smirked. "That will take the edge off! I guess we should be grateful that the cart didn't go into the ditch." His hand trembled when he held it to his lips. Some of the liquid dribbled down his cheek. He did not say anything else.

Andreas sat quietly next to Richard. There was nothing more to be done right now. He did not want to touch the leg and risk getting dirt into it. Flies tried to land on the leg, attracted by the smell of blood. Andreas used a switch to drive them away.

The sunlight crawled closer, and Andreas thought he would have to shift Richard again, when he heard the sounds of hooves in the distance.

Chapter 26

GEMMA RODE IN FRONT. HER CAP HAD FALLEN OFF, AND HER HAIR tumbled to her shoulders. Three men on mules followed her.

Gemma slipped off Hilde's back and knelt next to Richard. "I got help, Father."

Richard smiled at her weakly. "Good girl."

The three men dismounted. One of them walked with a severe limp. He was a young man, tall and skinny, with angular features and closely cropped dark curly hair. The two others were stockier in build and looked older.

Gemma said, "Andreas, this is Guido. He brought two of his people." She smiled at the two older men as she introduced them, "Bruno and Luca."

Guido, with a look of concern on his bony face, said something. Andreas could not understand his accent, but Gemma apparently had no difficulty.

"Andreas, do you think that we should hang the stretcher between the two mules?" She pointed at a rectangular object with four long handles tied to the back of one of the mules. It looked like a cross between a flattened-out basket and a wheelbarrow without wheels.

Andreas shook his head. "No, he'll be better off in the cart. But we could use the stretcher to get him from the tree into the cart."

Gemma talked to Guido and he, in turn, explained to the others. Andreas came close to laughing at this cumbersome relay of messages. The three men nodded eagerly and turned to Richard.

"Wait a moment," Andreas said. Then he climbed into the cart and cleared the space in the middle between the perches. "So, let's do it."

Richard looked up at them. He tried to grin. "It will be nice to get out of the sun."

They worked as carefully as they could, lifting Richard onto the stretcher and carrying him over to the cart. Richard was pale and sweating, his face frozen in a grimace to keep from groaning. They had to leave the door open, because the board was too long to fit inside. Andreas tied the door to the side of the cart so that it would not hit the board as the cart moved along.

Andreas mounted Hilde and led Trajan on a long rein. Gemma clucked to Paris and Helen, and they moved forward. Guido spoke to one of the servants, who nodded in response and rode ahead.

It was a slow procession. They made their way along the downward-slanting road, past fields and olive groves, and alongside a swiftly moving stream. Andreas was relieved when they finally reached a stone bridge and a farmhouse with a watermill on the other side, hugging the stream. The watermill turned slowly, trailing silvery drops of water. A small, wiry-looking elderly woman, dressed in a long black tunic with a black woolen scarf around her shoulders, stood in the farmyard and waved. She smiled at them and then bustled ahead to show the way into the kitchen, where she had already cleared the table.

Luca and Bruno, together with Andreas and Gemma, lifted Richard out of the cart and carried him into the kitchen.

"What do you want us to do now, Andreas?"

Andreas frowned. It felt strange to be giving orders. Then he put that thought out of his mind. "Gemma, do you remember the stuff your father used when I got hurt? Do you know if any is left?"

Gemma looked pale and worried. "Oh no! Father said the other day that he was hoping to get to a well-stocked monastery in order to get more of it!" Gemma bit her lip in consternation. "Isn't there anything else that would work?"

Andreas thought hard, trying to marshal a memory of Nicholas's supplies. "There are things one could use—myrrh, perhaps, and honey—hyssop would be good, also mint and thyme," he said slowly.

Gemma nodded. "I'm sure that they have all of that. What else?"

"Right now, we need hot water, clean rags, and chamomile tea.

Wine or something stronger would be helpful. I also need something to sew up the wound. Gemma, could you ask whether there is anything like catgut and a needle I could use— the finer the better?"

Gemma turned to the old woman and repeated the items that Andreas needed. When she got to the part about catgut, she did not know what the word in Italian might be and used signs to illustrate.

The old woman listened, peering Andreas with intense, alert, birdlike eyes. Then she responded in a rapid patter of words, so fast that Andreas gave up trying to understand. She clapped her hands, and a young servant girl rushed to fill a cast-iron pot with water. The old woman disappeared into the back of the house. Within moments, she returned, proudly bearing snowy white linen towels. They looked as if they had come out of someone's dowry chest.

Andreas moved to take the towels from her when he realized that his hands were filthy. "Sorry. I need to wash before I do anything."

The old woman nodded and spoke, but again too fast for Andreas to follow. Guido grinned. Clearly making an effort to slow down and speak clearly, he said, "Come, let me show you." He led Andreas to the scullery. "Don't worry. Nonna will get you everything you need."

"Nonna?" Andreas asked, scrubbing his hands vigorously. "My grandmother. She always has everything."

Indeed, Guido was right. She even produced catgut. Later, Andreas learned from Gemma that Guido's father used to repair string instruments and had always kept a supply of catgut in the house. He had died a few years ago.

Andreas studied his equipment; it would have to do. "What about a splint?" Gemma asked.

Andreas slapped his head. "How could I forget? We need to come up with something temporary to keep the leg secure for a few days until the wound has closed completely. Eventually, we can splint it properly."

Gemma had lost her pallor. She studied the leg thoughtfully. She turned to Guido and explained what was needed, after which

Guido, Bruno, and Luca talked at great speed. Andreas watched the excited back and forth with fascination. Finally, the two older men nodded and disappeared into the yard.

Then Andreas remembered something else. He looked at Guido. "Do you have some wine I could use?"

Nonna pulled on his arm. She held out a small clay jug, beaming with pride.

He sniffed at the clear liquid. "What is this?"

Guido laughed. "It's grappa—powerful stuff. We make it here; we use grape skin, seeds, and even the stems. It's very good. Just don't let Richard drink too much of it!"

"Oh, this is perfect," Andreas said. "I don't want him to drink it—though he might like it. I will use it to clean the needle and the catgut."

Andreas frowned as he looked at the twisted lower part of the shin, trying to visualize the way in which Nicholas had dealt with a broken arm. It had happened just once, but he remembered what Nicholas had told him about bones shortening as they healed if they were not set right.

"Richard, this will be the worst part. I need to straighten out the bones. I am sorry, it will hurt."

"Just get on with it," Richard grunted. Then he held up his hand. "May I have some of that grappa, before you start?"

Andreas nodded tensely. His face was damp with sweat. "I'll need help." He glanced up and found Guido beside him, looking at him calmly. He showed Guido where to hold Richard's leg. The next few minutes were agonizing. It was like trying to fit shards of pottery together in the dark. Mercifully, Richard fainted, which helped because he relaxed his muscles. When the leg was straight, it felt as if hours had gone by.

Andreas carefully cleaned and bathed the area around the wound with chamomile tea. Nicholas had said that deep wounds should not be closed completely. This one certainly was deep. After rinsing the catgut and the needle in the grappa, Andreas began to place stitches across the cut. It was hard, and he wished he had paid more attention to Gemma's sewing instructions on the road. Nonna peered over his shoulder while he worked. She muttered approvingly and seemed to know when to hold out the scissors or another clean rag.

Fortunately, Richard did not regain consciousness, until Andreas had finished placing stitches, and the leg was safely encased and completely immobilized in a complicated structure of padded, narrow, wooden boards, with an opening around the wound. He could only wiggle his toes.

Gemma laughed at him. "It looks like a cradle for your leg!" Richard was too exhausted to respond.

Eventually, everybody sat down at the kitchen table while Richard rested on a pallet in the room next to the kitchen. The table was filled with platters of food. Nonna kept encouraging Andreas and Gemma to eat, apparently worried that they might starve in front of her eyes. Bruno and Luca ate silently and voraciously. Luca had fed the birds, evidently pleased to be handling a gyrfalcon and a peregrine as well as a merlin. It turned out that he had some experience with kestrels and sparrow hawks. Gemma and Guido kept up a steady chatter. Andreas heard them as if through a haze.

Nonna stood up. "Come, you must rest now." She led him into a chamber and pointed out a pallet where he could sleep.

Andreas nodded, too tired to respond. He sat down. His last thought before he fell asleep was of Nicholas carefully threading a needle.

Andreas woke to the creaking sound of the watermill. He got up and looked out of the window. The water in the stream below was so clear that he could see the white pebbles on the bottom. He pulled on his tunic and went to the kitchen.

"Good morning!" Nonna beamed at him, and Andreas noticed that two of her front teeth were missing. It made her look even more birdlike.

"Thank you for your help last night!" Andreas said awkwardly.

Nonna waved her hands. "It's nothing. Go see him; he is waiting for you."

Richard was alert. He smiled at Andreas. "You did well yesterday. I am grateful."

Andreas blushed. "May I take a look at your leg?" "Go ahead. Feast your eyes on your handiwork."

Richard winced when Andreas peeled back the linen pieces. The leg looked swollen and uncomfortable. Some pus had drained out at the opening. Andreas would bathe it again with chamomile. He studied the rough stitches, definitely not like Gemma's neat work, but it would have to do. Gently, he replaced the linen covering.

"Get something to eat," Richard said abruptly.

Over the next two days, Andreas, Gemma, and Nonna took turns in carefully bathing Richard's leg. Nonna produced a salve for wounds. Andreas sniffed at it. Matilda used to make something out of yarrow and goldenrod. This seemed familiar. It could not hurt.

Richard was in pain and had a hard time sleeping. He looked irritable and tense, now that the first shock had worn off. But he submitted to Andreas's ministrations patiently and even obediently, even though it was clear that he fretted about being helpless.

Nonna cooked and cooked. She bustled about the house and the yard, trim and severe in her black tunic. Her smile and cheerful chatter made it clear how happy she was to have the house full.

Gemma spent a lot of time outside. Sometimes when checking on the birds, Andreas saw her sit with Guido on a little stone bench in the shade.

Occasionally, she came back excitedly to tell Richard and Andreas all about the farm. Guido's mother had died when he was born. He was born with a clubfoot. His grand-mother had raised him. Three years ago, his father died, leaving Guido the farm with the watermill. Bruno and Luca were distant cousins with no land of their own, so Guido's father had taken them in. Owning a watermill was a source of wealth in this region where any body of water represented a precious resource.

Richard raised his eyebrows when she relayed all this but did not comment. On the third day, when Gemma was outside, Richard said, "Andreas, pull up that chair. We need to talk."

Andreas sat down. All his confidence over the past few days fled in an instant. He picked up a rag that had fallen on the floor, rolling it up and flattening it out again.

Richard said, "You have told me that it would be a while

before I can walk or ride again."

Andreas opened his mouth to respond, but Richard stopped him. "Wait, I am not finished. I have worked it out with Guido. For the time being, we can stay here. But there is the matter of my report to Emperor Frederick, the news about Enzio, and the delivery of the gyrfalcon. This cannot wait. The emperor won't be at the castle indefinitely. You must do it."

"But what about Gemma? And if I go, I won't be able to help take care of you."

"Gemma is fine; I think she is quite content to tell you the truth. And as for taking care of me, now that the worst is over, I think that Nonna, Gemma, and Guido are more than enough to attend to the needs of a middle-aged man with a perfectly bandaged leg."

"I am afraid," Andreas confessed.

"You'll do fine. I'll tell you everything you need to know. You'll take the report and my trading permit for identification. All I ask is that you first deal with my deliveries before you address yourself to your own concerns."

Andreas swallowed. Richard was right; this was his opportunity.

Richard looked at him quizzically, then said, "You can do this. I trust you."

Chapter 27

ANDREAS SET OUT AT DAYBREAK. BRUNO AND LUCA HELPED TO GET the cart ready. Nonna handed him a basket with food for the road.

Gemma hugged him and whispered in his ear, "Thank you for taking care of my father! I hope you get what you want!"

Guido had told Luca to accompany Andreas for part of the way. Andreas was grateful for his company, silent though it was. Helen could not resist nipping Paris on the neck when they first began to move, but then both mules settled to their work. Andreas held the reins loosely; he needed to flick the whip only occasionally. He was free to look across the fields and at the castle in the distance. The closer they got, the greener the vegetation. Guido had told him that there were more sources of water in the region around the castle.

By the time they had covered half the distance, it was midmorning. Luca pulled up his mule. Andreas offered him some water, but Luca smiled at him and shook his head. His weathered brown face was seamed with laugh lines.

"Thank you, I am fine." He pointed at the dusty road that snaked its way through the plain and into a forest around the base of the castle. "This road goes all the way to the castle; you will be there by midday."

For a moment, Andreas wanted to plead with him to go on until they reached the castle. But he said nothing. Luca turned around, waved, and rode back the way they had come.

Andreas picked up the reins. Then, as the mules trotted along obediently, his mood shifted to a feeling of exhilaration. He had a gyrfalcon in the back, an important report in his satchel, and a sheaf of papers from King Enzio. He was going to meet the emperor. He would ask for sanctuary for Adela. A year ago, he had been hiding out in his little hut in the woods and stealing bread from the kitchen.

Andreas reached the woods that surrounded the castle. When he looked up and beyond the tree line, he could see the gleaming white towers that had given the structure its crown-like appearance from the distance. There were eight towers, each in the shape of an octagon. Richard had told him that the emperor had designed the castle himself. It did not look like any building Andreas had ever seen or could have imagined.

The road through the woods was shaded—a welcome change since the sun had reached its zenith. He breathed in the pungent scent of the pine trees. It was a much larger forest than he had realized. From the distance, it had looked like a thin green girdle surrounding the base of the castle. It took a long time to move through it. Andreas found his thoughts wandering, lulled by the droning of the cicadas all around him. Then he came out of the woods. The final stretch of the road leading up to the castle was on level ground. The white walls threw back the light from the sun, nearly blinding Andreas as he approached.

Two guards stood in front of the gate. One walked up to the side of the cart. "Are you lost?" He eyed the colorful cart and the dusty mules disdainfully.

"No," Andreas said, pulling out the trading permit with the imperial seal. "I am here on behalf of the trader Richard of Brugge. I am delivering a gyrfalcon for the emperor and a report that I must hand over in person."

The guard made a sign to him to wait. He stepped through the gate. A few moments later, he returned and said politely, "Come along. I will show you where to leave the cart."

Andreas was surprised at the ease with which he gained admittance. Richard must have developed a lot of credit with the emperor. Andreas drove the cart through the gate and pulled up. "Should I take the gyrfalcon out of the cart now?" he asked the guard.

The man shook his head. "No, please wait. We sent someone to inform the head falconer of your arrival. He will want to talk to you before inspecting the falcon."

While he waited, Andreas looked around and forgot all about his purpose for being there. The gate opened onto an octagonal courtyard, with eight doorways leading into the eight towers. It was like stepping into one of Brother Stefan's mathematical calculations. The blue-green mosaic tiles on the door-frames and mantelpieces stood out starkly against the light-colored marble columns and walls. Andreas glanced up at the sky. Dazzled by the brilliant light, he could no longer distinguish between the building and its surroundings. The sky had turned into a giant octagonal mosaic tile, rimmed by the white walls of the castle.

"We expected you earlier. Where is Master Richard? How is the gyrfalcon holding up?"

Andreas turned around. The speaker was a short, slightly built man, with a lined and weathered face. He wore simple, nondescript clothes, but his authority was evident.

"It was a long journey, and Master Richard had an accident. That's why he sent me in his place. The gyrfalcon is well. We have flown him regularly," Andreas responded politely.

The man raised his eyebrows. "We? Are you telling me that you have worked with the falcon? You look a bit young for this responsibility."

"Yes, it was important to keep him fit and healthy." Andreas was chagrined by the man's surprise that he had handled the falcon.

"When was he flown last?"

"Yesterday morning. I flew him to the lure only."

"Did you feed him today? What have you been feeding him?

When did he go into molt?" The questions went on for a while. "Well, then let's see him," the man said finally.

Andreas climbed into the cart. Adela did not stir. Andreas looked at the gyrfalcon in the dim light. Throughout the journey, he had not cared for him in the way that he cared for Adela. He admired him, he was fascinated by his cool pure splendor and remote bearing, but he did not love him. Yet, now Andreas felt sad to take him out of the cart for the last time.

"Well, old man, are you ready? I hope you do us proud."

Andreas was pleased to see that all the careful handling over the past months had paid off. The falcon was relaxed and willingly stepped onto Andreas's gloved arm. In the courtyard,

Andreas took off the falcon's hood.

The head falcon whistled softly when he saw the snowy white bird. He slowly walked around Andreas, looking at the falcon from all sides. Throughout, the gyrfalcon sat quietly on Andreas's arm; haughty and composed, he scanned the surroundings.

Finally, the head falconer beckoned to a young man standing behind him, who had watched everything attentively. "Nestore, I want you to take the falcon from Master Andreas. You will handle him for the time being."

Andreas felt his ears burn at being called Master Andreas. The transfer was smooth, and Nestore walked off with the falcon on his arm.

The head falconer watched him go and then turned back to Andreas. "You brought us a fine bird, and he looks like he is in excellent health. I can see that he has been handled well. I will report this to the emperor. I will take you to him now."

Chapter 28

THE HEAD FALCONER LED THE WAY TO THE CENTRAL TOWER ACROSS the courtyard. As Andreas followed him, he felt curiously detached as if he were watching himself climb up the wide stone staircase. He had dreamed of meeting the emperor for so long, imagining what it might be like, even talking to him in his dreams. Now the reality of it left him disoriented. Awed, he studied the vaulted ceiling of the large chamber on the second level and the arched window opening into the courtyard mirrored by a window on the opposite side. The room was spacious and bright. It also looked unfinished. In one corner, Andreas saw pieces of marble stacked up. One of the walls was lined with marble up to the windowsill, while the other walls were bare.

In the center of the room, a stout man in a simple gray tunic sat at a large table covered with scrolls and manuscripts. The man was nearly bald, with remnants of reddish-blond hair. The head falconer approached the table, bowed, and spoke in a low voice for a while. Then he came back to where Andreas waited and said quietly, "The emperor is ready to see you now."

Speaking in a formal tone, the head falconer announced, "Master Andreas, my lord."

Andreas was jolted into a state of panic; his earlier sense of detachment had vanished. He glanced around to see if the head falconer was still there. No, he was gone. Andreas squared his shoulders and walked up to the desk. He bowed awkwardly.

When Andreas raised his head, he looked into the face of a man well past his prime. It was a blunt face, with a strong chin and a sturdy straight nose. The green eyes were strained and red-rimmed.

Deep wrinkles were etched around the mouth and eyes; a ruddy skin tone spoke to a lot of time spent outdoors.

"Well, Master Andreas, I understand you brought us a fine gyrfalcon. I am pleased. I expect that you have a report from Master Richard." The emperor spoke in a baritone, his voice slightly hoarse, as if he was tired or ill.

Andreas pulled Richard's sealed roll out of his tunic. "Yes, my lord. Here is the report."

The emperor held out his hand. He broke the seal, flattened out the rolled up pages, and skimmed through them. "This is a very detailed report; I will read it carefully. Master Richard has never yet failed me. How long have you been on the road?"

"We have been traveling since May. That is, I joined Richard when he was at Castle Kragenberg."

"Castle Kragenberg, near Lübeck?" "Yes, my lord."

"Ah, now I remember, Count Cuno, isn't it? He is not a great friend of mine. But no matter. Master Richard vouched for you."

"My lord, I am also to tell you about Bologna." To his chagrin, Andreas was not able to control a slight stammer.

The emperor glanced at Andreas sharply. "Bologna?" Then he searched on his desk until he found a little bronze bell. He swung the bell, and a servant appeared. "Bring us some wine and water."

The servant bowed and disappeared. The emperor made a sign to Andreas to wait. Andreas looked at his dusty boots, trying to contain the fear welling up. In a few moments, the servant returned with two silver carafes and two goblets on a platter.

The emperor nodded. "That will do. Now leave us and close the door." Then he said to Andreas, "As it happens, my advisers are away and I am alone." He waved at the wine carafe. "Would you pour me some wine? You may take some if you wish. I see that you have had a long journey."

Andreas did as he was told, but refrained from pouring wine for himself. He felt like an impostor.

"Now talk. I can see from your face that it is not good news."

Andreas fumbled for words. "My lord, there was an attempt to free King Enzio, but the plan fell through."

The emperor sat still, his face masklike.

Andreas reached into his satchel and took out the sheaf of papers that Enzio had given to him. "King Enzio asked me to bring you this."

The emperor put the papers on the table without glancing at them. He stood up and walked to the window. Andreas watched the emperor's hunched back as he stared at the sundrenched golden green landscape below the castle. It made him think of a bird looking through bars of a cage. Then, the emperor turned around and came back to his chair. He sat down stiffly, moving like an old man. "I want you to tell me everything."

He proceeded to question Andreas about the details of the plan to free Enzio. When Andreas fell silent, the emperor picked up the sheaf of papers and started reading. Andreas could see him mouthing words. His face looked bleak. After a few moments, he refolded the papers carefully and placed them into a drawer.

"Master Andreas, I want to hear more about your journey."

Andreas was caught off guard by this shift in mood and the emperor's ability to put aside the personal. The emperor asked incisive questions about Goslar, Bamberg, Verona, Ferrara, and other cities they had passed through, the condition of the various regions, the indicators of trade, and the mood of the people. Andreas once again found reason to be grateful for Richard's relentless training; after he recovered from his initial nervousness, he was able to respond to most of the emperor's questions.

The emperor listened intently. Then he asked, "So, what do you think about it all—after everything you have seen on your journey from the north to Apulia? What do you think about the empire and its future?"

Andreas, for an instant, was transported back to the dark alley in Ferrara and the sound of a woman being brutally beaten. He could not very well talk about his disgust at some of the things he had seen and heard. "It is too big for me," he said carefully. "It seems as if there are many pieces that don't fit together."

The emperor looked at Andreas with an odd light in his eyes. "That's an interesting response." He reached over to a small pile of mosaic tiles in different colors and sizes on the desk. He picked up one tile and handed it to Andreas. "When I look at this, I know exactly what I want this building to look like when it is finished. Yet, when I leave here, I cannot always see it in my mind's eye."

Holding the blue tile in his hand, Andreas did not know whether he was expected to say anything.

The emperor continued speaking, softly as if he were alone. "What will be left behind when I am gone? I doubt that many of my buildings will remain or if so only the remnants." The emperor pointed at the tiles and the marble pieces. "People will come and strip these walls bare. Perhaps they will stop to admire the facilities for running water before stealing the tiles." He laughed— a discordant bark tossed back by the bare stone walls. Nothing had ever sounded so sad to Andreas as this laugh.

The emperor held up the report, tapping it with his finger. "You helped Richard collect a lot of this information. Now tell me a little about yourself. How did you end up with Richard?"

"I used to work in the mews at Castle Kragenberg. When Richard passed through the area, he needed an assistant."

The emperor looked curious. "I think there is more to this tale. It's odd—you remind me of myself when I was your age and roaming the streets of Palermo. Where are you headed after you leave here? Will you stay with Richard?"

"No, my lord." Andreas hesitated. Then he continued. "I want to become a healer."

The emperor nodded. "Go on, tell me more."

Andreas told the emperor about his weeks with Nicholas, reading in Trotula's manuscript, and Richard's accident. "I think I can do this. I could become a good healer."

The emperor smiled. "You might be interested to know that there are many healers like Trotula at the medical school in Salerno. Some of them come to my court to talk about their research." He fixed his stern gaze on Andreas. "I don't need to tell you that you will have to work hard to achieve your goal. There are no shortcuts."

"Yes, I know, my lord." Andreas cleared his throat, twisting the blue tile around and around in his hand. Then he held it up so the blue glazing glowed in the light from the window. "This tile makes me think of the things people have tried to teach me— the symmetry of the human body and the need for balance." In his intent to explain, he forgot to whom he was talking. "I think illness is a kind of imbalance; healing would be about restoring balance. I want to learn how to do that."

"Medicine and falconry are not all that different," the emperor said thoughtfully. "A good falconer has to deal with balance all the time—balance of exercise and rest, balance in the feeding, and most of all balance in the emotions—control and freedom, speed and patience. It seems to me a good basis for learning to become a healer."

He turned to his desk. Impatiently, he searched among the papers, dropping some on the floor. Andreas saw a drawing of a building overlaid with complicated mathematical formulas. The writing on another sheet looked like a list. The emperor's intentness reminded Andreas of Enzio's passionate absorption in his poetry.

"Look, here are notes for an addition to my book about falcons. It deals with methods of healing and medicine for birds of prey. You might find this interesting. It is based on research I have done and have collected over the years. It took too long, but it's worth it."

Andreas studied the pages, intrigued by the sketches of birds that accompanied them. He saw headings such as "The treatment of intestinal disorders in falcons" and "How to distinguish disease from the results of emaciation or mishandling of falcons."

Then, the emperor spoke again, but so low that Andreas could barely hear him. "This is what might survive—ideas and thoughts." Slowly, he gathered the papers into a neat pile.

Then, he raised his head and looked at Andreas. "You told me what you have done on our behalf and on King Enzio's behalf, and I honor you for that. Now, it is time for me to return to my work and for you to return to your master. Is there anything else?"

This was the moment. If Andreas wanted to ask about Adela, he had to do it now. He looked at the stern, imperious man at his desk, infinitely weary and sad.

"Well?"

"No, my lord," Andreas said.

The emperor picked up a quill and dipped it into an inkwell. With quick, sure strokes, he wrote a few lines on a piece of parchment. He folded it and wrote a name on top. He held some sealing wax over a candle, dropped the wax on the paper, and pressed his ring onto the wax. Then he reached into a drawer and pulled out something small that he placed into a little felt bag.

"Here, take this as a token of my gratitude. And this"—he held out the paper to Andreas—"is a letter to someone I know in the town of Salerno. I suggest that before you make any decisions about your future, you have a talk with him. The head falconer will give you something for your master."

Andreas bowed. A servant took him back to the yard where the cart was. The mules had been watered and fed. The head falconer shook his hand, and then Andreas was already through the gate; it closed behind him.

PART VIII

PARTINGS AND BEGINNINGS

On Retrieving a Nomadic Falcon

"[The falconer] must call to her and wave his glove in an attempt to recall her. If she does not then return to her proper position above him, he must leave his companion, if he has one, and himself follow the falcon, calling her with the proper cries. The mere fact of his presence may bring her above the falconer's head. Even when he has no assistant, he must nevertheless follow the falcon, but not at a rapid gait, because the falcon is flying slowly, and there is no need to ride fast after her; he must be careful only not to lose sight of her. It happens frequently, since the falcon is not chasing a bird, that she will come back at the sound of the falconer's voice or at the sight of the waving glove."

- Frederick von Hohenstaufen, The Art of Falconry, being the De Arte Venandi cum Avibus, of Frederick II of Hohenstaufen

Chapter 29

THE CART ROLLED ALONG ON THE DUSTY ROAD AWAY FROM THE castle.

Andreas sat on the bench and stared at the mules' sturdy backs without seeing anything at all.

Suddenly, the light shifted; he had reached the wooded area. The road was covered with pine needles, and the cart made almost no sound at all. After a while, a clearing opened up in front of him. The track led straight across a meadow. Brambles and wild rosebushes in bloom surrounded the clearing. He could hear the soft murmuring of a stream nearby.

Andreas pulled up and got out of the cart. The mules looked at him balefully, unsure of what was happening. He scratched Paris on his forehead. Helen laid her ears back. "I know—you don't like being scratched. Guess what? We will rest here for a while."

He led them to a tree in the shade. He took the wooden bucket from the cart and went to the stream. He rinsed his face and arms and then filled the bucket. The mules had been fed at the castle, so this would have to be enough to tide them over until he brought them back to the farm. He checked to see what was in the basket Nonna had packed for him. It was perfect—filled with bread, cheese, roasted meat, and a flask with wine.

Andreas had not been on his own like this since his days in his hut in the forest at Castle Kragenberg. He sat down, leaning against a tree trunk. A large bird circled overhead. Andreas followed it with his eyes until it was gone. He sat quietly, the only sounds the snuffling of the mules and birds in the distance.

He pulled out the emperor's letter and studied the name on it, Mahir Ibn Ghaiyyas in Salerno. He decided against opening the little bag. It felt like a ring. He would show it to Richard. But there was something else—the blue tile from the castle. Andreas rubbed the edges of the tile, turning it around and around in his hand.

Almost a year had gone by since the day he hid Adela in the little hut in the woods. He had promised her that he would take care of her. Now she sat in a dark cart by the roadside. He had been convinced that Adela would find a new home in the emperor's mews and hunt with the emperor as befitted her station. Oswald had warned him. Richard also had warned him in his indirect way of speaking. Even Enzio had expressed his doubt. Andreas had not believed them.

Only once he stood in front of the emperor, had he finally understood that he could not ask the emperor for sanctuary. It would have been wrong. The emperor could not have acted against his own laws just as Oswald could not have disobeyed a direct order from his lord.

He knew what Emperor Frederick II would have said. It was as Andreas had heard him, speaking with his hoarse deep voice, "I am bound by the same laws as everyone else. I expect obedience to my decrees. I cannot bend them to my convenience or my whim. The falcon transgressed against its lord, and its life is forfeit. The one who took the falcon in disregard of the owner's decree committed a crime; and his life too is forfeit or subject to a grave penalty."

For a moment, Andreas smiled. There was an easy solution to his problems. He could take up the offer of that count outside of Verona. Something told him that the count would not be overly concerned with whether or not a falcon had been stolen as long as it would make a nice addition to his collection of hunting birds and beautiful objects. Andreas shook his head. This was all behind him.

Again, as so many times before, he thought of the tapestry with its glowing world of knights, falconers, and falcons in Castle Kragenberg. Adela no longer belonged in that tapestry and nor did he.

He stood up. He was content. He had made his decision.

It was late afternoon by the time Andreas got back to the farm. Gemma sat on the stone steps outside the kitchen with a large bowl in front of her, shelling peas. She looked up and beamed at him. "Andreas! How did it go? Did you see the emperor?"

"Everything went well. How is Richard?"

Gemma made a face. "Cranky! I feel like dumping cold water on him half of the time."

"I will go to him as soon as I have taken care of the mules." Andreas hopped off the cart.

"Let me help you. The peas can wait." Gemma came over and began to free Helen from the traces.

Andreas was grateful that Gemma did not ask any other questions. She hummed cheerfully to herself as she helped him take the mules to the stable.

"Where is Guido?" Andreas asked. "He is doing the accounts."

"The accounts?" Andreas asked curiously.

"Yes, for the mill. It's the only mill in the area, and he has a lot of business. So he has to keep track of everything." The note of pride in Gemma's voice intrigued Andreas, but he was too tired to pursue it. Once the mules had been watered and fed, Andreas went to the house.

The kitchen smelled of fresh bread, and a large pot with a savory soup of barley, onions, and herbs simmered on the hearth. Ducking his head to avoid hitting the doorframe, Andreas went into the room where Richard stayed. He looked disgruntled and uncomfortable. His beard was untrimmed, and his hair stuck up in all directions. At the sight of Andreas, his face brightened.

"Ah, you are back! How did it go?"

"It went well. The head falconer liked the falcon. I delivered your report to the emperor. He gave me a purse for you." Andreas handed it to Richard.

"And?" Richard asked. "That's all you are going to tell me?"

"Right now it is. Let me look at your leg."

"Oh, if you must. I'm sick of this—Gemma and Nonna treat me like a baby. I'm not allowed to do anything. I can't do this, I can't do that. Do this, do that, drink this, eat that—all day long!"

Andreas hid a grin. He peeled back the padding and studied the wound. "It's healing well."

Richard grunted. Then he said, "You look like you are about to fall asleep. Go on, get some food, and talk to me tomorrow."

Andreas nodded. He was not yet ready to talk about what had happened. All of a sudden, he could barely keep his eyes open.

Without bothering about food, he went directly to the chamber he shared with Bruno and Luca and lay down.

Chapter 30

WHEN ANDREAS WOKE UP, HE WAS DISORIENTED. HE MUST have slept through the night. He walked out of the house into a brilliant early summer morning.

The meadow above the stream looked odd—a portion of it seemed to be dotted with white flat cakes. Then, he saw Gemma shaking out linen sheets and spreading them on the grass to bleach in the sunlight. Guido sat on a tree trunk on the edge of the meadow, his face turned toward Gemma. Occasionally, she glanced at him and smiled. Andreas turned and went back to the kitchen.

Nonna had put out some bread and ale on the table. Andreas was ravenous. He sat down and ate, listening to the swishing sounds in the back of the house, Nonna at work with her straw broom. He wondered whether this frail-looking old woman ever slept. When he was done, he went to check on Richard.

Richard looked less disgruntled this morning. He had devised a means to scratch his leg in the area underneath the makeshift splint, energetically poking at it with a long quill. "Well, good morning! It's about time. Are you ready to tell me a bit more about yesterday?"

"Let me look at your leg first," Andreas said. When he was done, he sat down. "Tomorrow, we can splint it properly, and I'll talk to Guido about getting you a set of crutches."

Richard waved his hand impatiently. "Yes, yes, but first I want to know about yesterday."

Andreas described his encounter with the emperor.

Richard looked thoughtful. "I know that things are not looking too good for Emperor Frederick. The report was hardly likely to cheer him up. But I must say I envy you. It seems he talked to you more than he ever talked to me. And Adela?"

Andreas watched the dust motes that swirled around in the

sunlight streaming in from the window. He could hear the rhythmic creak of the watermill. "I couldn't do it. I didn't ask him." He raised his head, looking directly at Richard. "It would have been all wrong. I could not ask him to go against his own laws. I suddenly understood what you and Oswald and even Enzio had been telling me."

"But I never said anything."

"True, but you made me think. Also, it seemed wrong to exploit his gratitude for our attempt to free Enzio." Andreas paused and then added, "I felt sorry for him. In a way, he is a prisoner just as much as Enzio."

Richard's eyes were shining. "What will you do now?"

Andreas said, "I want to take her further inland where there are few villages and release her."

Richard was quiet. He used the quill to draw imaginary patterns on the blanket. Then he said, "For what it's worth, I think this is right. This is a good area for a young falcon in the summer. By the fall, she will be ready to go further south. She will do well."

Andreas nodded. After a moment, he took out the letter from the emperor together with the little pouch.

"The emperor gave me this letter to deliver." He held out the sealed envelope.

Richard read the inscription and raised his eyebrows. "Interesting."

"Do you know who that is?" Andreas asked eagerly. "Oh yes, I do."

"Tell me."

Richard grinned at Andreas. "By no means, young man. The emperor did not tell you, so it is not right that I should. But let me see what else you have there."

Andreas opened the little bag and pulled out the ring.

With raised eyebrows, Richard studied the intricate silver work, framing six small rubies and a pearl in the center. "Byzantine for sure. This is a substantial gift. You best keep it hidden in a safe place."

"Would you keep it for me?"

"It won't do you any good sitting in one of my little boxes.

No, I have a better idea. I can give you the name of a reputable banker and merchant who could sell this for you and then guide you with regard to the money from the sale. I will write to him and explain."

"But I can't sell this!"

"You most certainly can—that's why the emperor gave it to you—provided that you make intelligent use of it. Of course, if you waste it on fripperies, it would be a shame. By the way, when are you planning to leave?"

Andreas studied Richard's toes sticking out at the bottom of the pallet. He had not known how to broach this subject.

"Come now, you can't stay here twiddling your thumbs forever!" "I feel bad leaving you here when you are not yet able to walk after all you have done for me."

"As to that, young man, I might say that what you have done for me more than evens the score; so let's not quibble about that. I take it you are going to Salerno."

Andreas nodded. "I have thought about it since I met Nicholas. But I wasn't sure." The words spilled out faster and faster. "Now I am. I don't know how, but it will work out. I will try to work for someone at the university. Maybe I can become an apprentice to a physician. I want to study at the university."

"That sounds like an excellent plan. I also have had some time to think about things, and you may have noticed that there is another unexpected development."

Andreas looked up, distracted from his thoughts. Then he said carefully, "Gemma?"

"Right. Gemma. Guido came to me yesterday and asked for her hand in marriage. It seems fitting, and Gemma is happy. Some fathers might balk at a son-in-law with a clubfoot, but it does not seem to keep him from running his farm and mill. I certainly don't believe the local gobbledygook about the evil eye having done this to him. So, it looks as if Gemma is settled."

"And you?" Andreas asked.

"The truth is I don't know yet. I will make that decision in a month or so when I am able to move again. I have my eye on some olive groves in the area. Then again, I might decide to go to Palermo. Anyway, it need not concern you." Richard looked at

Andreas sternly. "Meanwhile, for you, the time has come to strike out on your own."

Chapter 31

A FEW DAYS LATER, ANDREAS WAS READY.

Richard had helped him to choose a good area for releasing the falcon. "Here," he said, pointing to a spot on the crude map he had drawn for Andreas, "there is a range of hills, perfect for birds of prey. It is about three hours west from here. There are no larger settlements nearby."

"I will leave in the afternoon and spend the night in the open, so I can release her early in the morning. Then she has all day to get her bearings and find a place to perch at night."

"Perhaps you should ask Bruno or Luca to come along," Richard said.

Andreas shook his head. "No, I need to do this by myself. I got her into this; it's my responsibility to see it through."

On the last day before Andreas planned to leave, Nonna had prepared a pot of barley stew, fennel and mushrooms fried in oil, and a fresh loaf of crusty bread baked with fennel seeds. They all sat at the table in the kitchen, talking and laughing as they ate. It was a hot day, but the stone walls of the farmhouse kept the rooms cool.

Finally, Richard pushed away his plate with a satisfied sigh. "Nonna, if you keep preparing so much lovely food, you will soon have to roll me out of here!"

Nonna smiled at him. "Eat, eat! It's good for you."

In honor of the occasion, Guido brought out some grappa, carefully pouring small amounts into little beakers. Richard sat with his leg stretched alongside the table, a pair of crutches on the floor next to him. Andreas was pleased with the crutches. It had taken some time to get them right. The first attempt had failed; the crutches broke when Andreas tested them. The second set was strong enough. Bruno filed the wood to remove all splinters. Andreas got some rags from Nonna to create padding on top.

Richard was still awkward in handling them, but improved every time he made his way around the house.

Andreas cleared his throat, praying that he was not wrong in his calculation. "Guido, please don't take this the wrong way. Would you show me your foot?"

Startled, Guido shook his head.

Gemma said, "Ah, Guido, let Andreas take a look. He is not likely to throw stones at you or call you devil's spawn. He just wants to help."

Reluctantly, Guido allowed Andreas to slip off his misshapen boot. Andreas ran his hands over the foot and gently manipulated it; it looked sore and swollen in areas where the boot chafed it. Then he sat back on his heels. "Guido, was it like this when you were born?"

Guido shrugged helplessly. He looked distraught and embarrassed at the attention.

But Nonna, watching everything with her bright bird eyes, said, "I'm not sure. I didn't notice anything wrong. You see Guido's mother died in childbirth. Guido's father was . . . well, he got into the grappa more than he should have. I was working to keep everything going, and we did not have any help in those years."

"Oh, Nonna, this is all so long ago! What good will all this talking do?" Guido protested. He tried to pull his foot out of Andreas's grasp.

Nonna swatted at him like an annoying fly. "No, let me finish. Perhaps this will help." She turned back to Andreas. "The fact is that Guido spent a lot of time in his crib; nobody had time for him. He was a quiet lad; he never cried. Finally, I got some help in the house. Later, we could all see there was a problem. People talked about witchcraft and pointed fingers at Guido's mother. You know how it is. Poor Guido! I caught kids throwing things at him and making fun of him." Nonna patted Guido on the back. "Once he got to be taller, they left him alone."

Andreas turned his attention back to Guido's foot. He pushed and pulled on it gently, shifting it slightly in different directions.

Guido winced but did not try to pull away.

Gemma brushed her hair out of her face. "What do you think, Andreas?"

Andreas, still studying Guido's foot and rubbing it, said slowly, "Look, Guido, I don't want to promise anything, but I think you can make this better or at least less uncomfortable."

"How?" Gemma and Guido spoke at the same time.

"It looks as if you did not use the foot enough when you were little. Maybe it got twisted when you were born, and then it couldn't grow and develop muscles. Nonna, do you use anything for when your bones hurt or your muscles are sore?"

Nonna shook her head.

"See if you can get hold of"—Andreas turned to Gemma—"I don't remember the word for hyssop. You make a poultice out of it. And beeswax and lemon balm for a salve."

Gemma explained to Nonna what was wanted. Nonna nodded eagerly.

"And then?" Gemma asked.

"Start by soaking the foot in warm water. After that, apply a hot poultice of hyssop. When it's nice and relaxed, move it with your hand as much as you can bear, gently stretching and stretching, a little bit every day, and massage the foot with lemon balm and beeswax. You need to construct a temporary brace to hold the foot in place, until the muscles stretch and are stronger. Once you have gotten the foot straightened out as much as possible, the best would be some sort of solid shoe or boot. It will take a while, and you have to be patient, but I think it will get better. Besides"—Andreas grinned at Guido affectionately—"you will have the cleanest foot in all of Apulia!"

Gemma and Guido looked at him with a mixture of fascination and hope; red spots of excitement appeared on Nonna's sallow, wrinkled cheeks. Richard's dour features were transformed by a satisfied smile.

"Where did you get all that from?" Gemma asked.

Andreas blushed. "Oh, when I was with Nicholas, he showed me some things," he mumbled. "Anyway, try it. It can't hurt."

Nonna got up. "Why don't we start today? Beeswax is not a problem. My son used that when he repaired string instruments. And we grow lemon balm and hyssop in the kitchen garden." She rushed off.

Bruno, who had listened silently, now said something, speaking so fast that Andreas could not follow and needed Gemma's help. "He said he could make a temporary brace out of an open shoe with a band that one could keep tightening every few days."

Andreas nodded gratefully. "That's it. You might have to experiment with it."

Guido looked sad. "I always thought my foot was a punishment for my mother dying when I was born. I am used to it."

Gemma smiled at him. "We will do this every single day! When you come back to visit, you can see how far we have gotten." She hugged Andreas. "Thank you, little brother!"

Chapter 32

THE NEXT MORNING, ANDREAS SET OUT, WITH ADELA IN HER basket and his belongings strapped behind him on Hilde's broad back.

Richard had offered that Andreas take Hilde. The saddlebags were filled with provisions for the first few days on the road. Richard handed Andreas some money to tide him over until Salerno. When Andreas protested, Richard scowled at him. "You earned it. Be quiet."

Bruno had patched up the old travel basket for Adela. In his pack, Andreas carried a little jar filled with a salve made of honey, yarrow, and rosemary from Nonna and a small flask of grappa from Guido.

Gemma had given him a pair of knitting needles. She grinned at him. "Keep practicing."

As Andreas rode under the bright blue Apulian sky past scrubby brush, fragrant with wild thyme and mint, he remembered how he used to stand in front of the tapestry at Castle Kragenberg and imagine himself in the emperor's train, with a falcon on his arm. Then he shook his head and laughed; it had been a wonderful dream. Hilde's ears twitched as she trotted along the sandy path.

By the time he reached the hills, the shadows had lengthened. He continued upwards until he reached an opening in the forest growth. These woods were perfect for his plan. They provided plenty of prey for Adela, safe trees for perching at night, and a wide-open landscape nearby to explore.

He drank from the flask that Nonna had given him and ate a piece of bread, chewing thoughtfully while working out his plan.

Everything Andreas had learned from Oswald and Richard had to do with how to recall falcons. Oswald always said, "The true art of falconry is the falconer's ability to let a falcon have its freedom and then have it return willingly and effortlessly to captivity."

None of Oswald's lessons had dealt with letting falcons go. Once he had mentioned that some lords regularly released falcons into the wild after a few years, but Andreas had not bothered to ask about it; it had not seemed important at the time. It occurred to Andreas that he had never asked Oswald much of anything. He had just been happy to be in the mews, watching Oswald with his swollen, knobby hands handle birds with firmness and understanding, listening to his stories about knights and falconry, and free to dream.

Now, Andreas had to figure out by himself how to do this. Normally, when hunting with a falcon, it was better to feed the bird only a little bit or nothing before the hunt. A hungry bird is more likely to return to the lure in anticipation of feed from the handler. Andreas decided to feed Adela in the morning so that she would be satiated and inclined to ignore him.

He settled down for the night, rolling out a blanket from his pack on a flat piece of ground. At first light, he woke up. He wanted everything to be ready. He packed up and saddled Hilde. Then he opened the basket. The young falcon looked plump, glossy, and fit.

"Well, my lady, we have come to the end of the road." He offered Adela scraps of feed that he had brought along. She grabbed them, swallowing everything rapidly; then she sat quietly again, confident and unafraid.

Andreas spoke to her as he had always done, in an easy relaxed voice. "No more traveling in a little cart for you. Today, you will fly as high as you want. Maybe you will meet some brothers and sisters. You will finally get to do what you do best. You'll see."

In Bologna, Umberto had spoken of Enzio's "gilded cage." Perhaps Adela had lived in a gilded cage as well—fed regularly, protected against the elements, and not exposed to other predators. Now she would be free—no longer at the whim of any lord, not even the emperor, no longer forced to live in someone else's dream.

Andreas thought of running his hand over her back and wings, but stopped at the last instant.

"A falcon is not a lap dog. It is a wild animal. Never forget that!" Oswald had told him over and over again.

It was time. Andreas secured the leather glove on his arm and put out his arm. Adela stepped onto it willingly. He slipped the hood over her head and began to walk up the narrow deer trail, careful to keep his arm steady so that she would be relaxed and calm.

He quickly reached the top. The tree growth had thinned out, and he could look into the plain below and the range of hills along its edge. Andreas waited, watching the sky and the trees around him. For a moment, he thought about flying Adela and recalling her one more time. No, Adela was going to need all her energies in the next few hours. He pulled off the long jesses on her ankles so that they would not become a source of danger to her in the wild and removed the little bell attached to her left foot just above the jess.

A large bird flew across the sky in the distance. Andreas lost sight of it again. Perhaps it was a falcon. He did not know how territorial other hunting birds would be. In any event, there was not much he could do about it; it would be up to Adela. If all went well, Adela would eventually find a mate. Oswald had told Andreas that falcons mate for life.

A flock of small birds swept across the tree line. Andreas took the falcon's hood off. He could sense her mounting excitement as she scanned her surroundings. He relished the firm grip of her talons on his arm. Once more, Andreas looked at the impenetrable, shiny black eyes, the shimmering white feathers setting off the sharp bars on her chest, and the luminous blue of her legs. Then he lifted his arm and gently launched her into the air.

Adela rose swiftly, climbing higher and higher, her wing-beat steady and powerful. She swooped and circled, scanning the area for prey. Something must have caught her attention beyond the tree line, because she banked sharply. Andreas followed her with his eyes as she headed toward the range of hills in the south. Then she was gone.

Andreas gazed into the distance. His throat hurt. He wanted to cry, and yet he had never in his entire life been quite as exhilarated as when he watched Adela take off into the morning sky.

With a sigh, he turned away. Adela must not see him if she circled the area again. Quickly, he ran down the hill where Hilde stood in the shade of a tree, peacefully swishing her tail. Within a few moments, he had crossed the clearing and was out of sight beneath the shady cover of the trees.

The little bell in his purse shifted, and he heard a muffled tinkle. He rubbed his hand over his eyes. Suddenly, he remembered Enzio's voice:

It flies far away to claim its dominion,
sailing to its castle in the middle of the blue sea,
the little falcon, and the sky overflows with joy.

"Go claim your dominion, my lady," Andreas whispered. He picked up the reins and headed west, toward Salerno.

EPILOGUE

SALERNO, YEAR OF THE LORD, JANUARY 1251

Dear Nicholas,

I hope this letter reaches you in good health. I did what you told me to do. I finished what I started. It turned out different from what I imagined, but perhaps you knew that already.

You can write to me care of Mahir Ibn Ghaiyyas, physician and professor at the Scuola Medica of Salerno. I found out that his name means 'The able, skillful one, son of the helper and reliever.' Isn't that a good name for a doctor?

I live in Dottore Ibn Ghaiyyas's home, a villa on a hill at the edge of town. His family makes me laugh a lot. They bicker and argue and joke and laugh all day long. His wife paints miniatures for books. One of his sons runs a pottery workshop. His oldest son, Sulaiman, manages the household. He is a wonderful cook.

They gave me a room all to myself. I can see the harbor from the window. Your amber stone hangs on a leather string in front of the window, and the blue tile from Castel del Monte is on my desk.

The doctor's wife never noticed that I started to live there until about two months had gone by. She met me in the hallway and asked in a dreamy voice what my name was. I told her I was working for her husband, but she had already lost interest. "That's nice," she said kindly. "Make sure Sulaiman feeds you properly." Her fingers are always covered with paint stains. I do not think she notices anything around her at all other than her husband and her work. Her face lights up when her husband comes into a room.

I have started attending lectures at the university. There is so much to learn. There is someone who gives lessons about performing experiments in order to determine whether a treatment works. Dottore Ibn Ghaiyyas lectures on the importance of a clean environment as well as clean tools. Oswald would like that. Then there is something called peer review of doctors' work by a medical council and the need for doctors to always keep a record of everything they do when treating someone.

I have to study Arabic, because a lot of important work in medicine was done by Muslim physicians like Ibn alNafis who researched the way blood flows throughout the body or Ibn Sina who talked about disease transmitted through the air. I wish I could show you some of the manuscripts from the library. Did you know that one of the founders of the university was called Adela the Arab? I was told there were four founders altogether—the Jewish physician Helinus, the Greek Pontus, the Arab Adela, and the Latin Salernus. For some reason, it makes me think of the eight towers of Emperor Frederick's castle.

When I am not at the university, I work as Dottore Ibn Ghaiyyas's assistant. The things you taught me are very useful. I have helped with two deliveries. Once I was allowed to watch during a surgery.

Dottore Ibn Ghaiyyas said the other day, 'You might make a passable doctor one day.'"

I already wrote to you about meeting the emperor and what I did with Adela. I want to tell you something that I have not told anybody else. In December, I went into the hills. Dottore Ibn Ghaiyyas had given me a free day, and I went to look for myrtle, juniper berries, and wild fennel. I sat on a rock in the winter sunlight and thought of everything that had happened in the last year. And then I saw a huge gyrfalcon. It cruised gently as if it were waiting for something. It was perfect, pure white, a winter dream. I wanted to weep, though I did not know why. Afterward, as if beckoned by an unheard call from far away, the falcon rose higher, turned abruptly, and flew off toward the east with a speed that defied description. Something had happened. Have you ever had a premonition? I just knew.

You know already what happened that day. You will have received messages probably even before we did in Salerno. I found out a week after my excursion into the mountains. Emperor Frederick died on December 13 at Castel Fiorentino in Apulia. He probably would have preferred to die at Castel del Monte. But we cannot choose the hour or the place of our death. I thought about that gyrfalcon for a long time. Perhaps it was the emperor's soul that took to the skies.

Of course, that falcon was not Adela. But in its fierce wild pride, it carried some of my dreams on its wings. I will never see Adela again. I am sad and I am happy all at the same time. Is it always like that? I have no regrets."

NOTES TO READER

Historical figures

Adela of Normandy (c. 1062-March 8, 1137), by marriage Countess of Blois, Chartres, and Meaux, a daughter of William the Conqueror and Matilda of Flanders. She was said to have been a high-spirited and educated woman, with some knowledge of Latin, who repeatedly acted as regent for her husband.

Enzio, king of Sardinia (c. 1218-1272), the eldest of the illegitimate sons of Frederick II of Hohenstaufen. He was said to have had a pleasant personality and a strong physical resemblance to his father. As a military leader, he fought alongside his father in many conflicts involving the Guelphs and the pope. During a campaign to support the Ghibelline cities of Modena and Cremona against Bologna, he was defeated and captured at the Battle of Fossalta on May 26, 1249. Enzio was imprisoned in Bologna. Every attempt to rescue him failed, and he died in prison in 1272, the last of the Hohenstaufen dynasty. Nicknamed Falconello, which means "little falcon" in Italian, Enzio shared his father's passion for falconry. He wrote many poems during the years of his imprisonment and together with his father was among the founding members of the Sicilian School of Poetry. He is rumored to have had several relationships while in prison, in particular, with one Lucia da Viadagola, a peasant.

Frederick I of Hohenstaufen (Barbarossa) (c. 1122-June 10, 1190), Holy Roman Emperor and king of Germany, Italy, and Burgundy. Barbarossa means "red beard" in Italian.

Frederick II of Hohenstaufen (December 26, 1194-December 13, 1250), Holy Roman Emperor and king of Germany, Italy, and Burgundy. His other titles were king of Sicily and king of Jerusalem.

He was frequently at war with the papacy and was excommunicated four times. He was said to have spoken six languages: Latin, Sicilian, German, French, Greek, and Arabic. By contemporary standards, Frederick II was an uncommonly avid patron of science and the arts. A poet himself, he was also a patron of the Sicilian School of Poetry. He founded the University of Naples and the medical school at Salerno, where women were admitted as teachers and students. In Sicily and southern Italy, Frederick II created a legal code for his realm that was remarkable for its time; it provided the foundation for a centrally governed kingdom with an efficient bureaucracy. With relatively small modifications, the Liber Augustalis remained the basis of Sicilian law until 1819.

Guelphs and **Ghibellines** were factions supporting the papacy and the Holy Roman Emperor, respectively, in central and northern Italy during the twelfth and thirteenth centuries. The name *Guelph* came from the family name of the dukes of Bavaria, the Welfs, who were opposed to the Hohenstaufens. The Hohenstaufen supporters, with their battle cry "Waiblingen," the name of a Hohenstaufen castle in Swabia, became known as the Ghibellines. Italian city-states were divided in their loyalty. Some sided with the Ghibellines and supported the emperor while others supported the pope and the Guelphs, notably in the allegiance known as the Lombard League. Broadly speaking, the Guelphs tended to come from wealthy mercantile families, whereas the Ghibellines were predominantly those whose wealth was based on agricultural estates. Adherence to one party or another could be motivated by local or regional political reasons and shifted in correspondence with political developments and upheavals.

Henry II (May 6, 973-July 13, 1024), Holy Roman Emperor, king of Germany, and king of Italy.

Henry VI (November 1165-September 28, 1197), Holy Roman Emperor, king of Germany, and king of Sicily.

The **Holy Roman Empire,** a complex political union of territories in Central Europe that was in existence from 962 to 1806. The territories making up the empire lay predominantly in Central Europe. At its peak in 1050, it included the Kingdom of Germany, the Kingdom of Bohemia, the Kingdom of Italy, and the Kingdom of Burgundy.

The **Lombard League** was an alliance formed in 1167. At its apex, it included most of the cities of northern Italy, including Bergamo, Cremona, Genoa, Bologna, Lodi, Milan, Modena, Padua, Reggio Emilia, Treviso, Venice, Verona, Vicenza, and even some lords, such as the Marquis Malaspina and Ezzelino III da Romano of Parma, although its membership changed with time. The Lombard League was one of the most formidable adversaries of Frederick II, always striving to counter his efforts to expand the power of the Holy Roman Empire in Italy. The league was dissolved after the death of Frederick II.

Lucia da Viadagola, a *contadina* (peasant woman) in Bologna in the thirteenth century, said to have had an affair with Enzio and produced a child as a result. According to the legend, Enzio used to say to Lucia, "*Amor mio, ben ti voglio,*" which means "My dear heart, I love you well" in Italian. This *ben ti voglio* is said to be the origin of the Bentivoglio family name. First recorded in Bologna in 1323, the Bentivoglio family belonged to one of the workingmen's guilds in the city. It became one of the most powerful Bolognese families in the fourteenth and fifteenth centuries. It contracted alliances with the kings of Aragon, the dukes of Milan, and other sovereigns.

Trotula of Salerno (d. 1097) was a female physician, alleged to have been the first female professor of medicine, teaching in the southern Italian town of Salerno, at that time the most important center of medical learning in Europe. In medieval Europe, her *Passionibus Mulierum Curandorum (The Diseases of Women)* was considered a major source of information on the treatment of women. It included information on conception, pregnancy, and childbirth, and stressed the importance of a healthy diet, exercise, and cleanliness. Her *Practicum Secundum Trota (Practical Medicine According to Trotula)* contained more general medical information.

SUGGESTED READINGS

Armstrong, Karen (2001). *Holy War – The Crusades and Their Impact on Today's World.* New York: Anchor Books, 2001.

Bishop, Morris. *The Middle Ages.* New York: American Heritage, Inc., 1996.

Cassady, Richard F. *The Emperor and the Saint: Frederick II of Hohenstaufen, Francis of Assisi, and Journeys to Medieval Places.* DeKalb: Northern Illinois University Press, 2011.

Davis, R.H.C. *A History of Medieval Europe.* New York: Routledge, 2013.

Dawson, Ian. *Medicine in the Middle Ages.* New York: Enchanted Lion Books, 2005

Frederick II of Hohenstaufen. *The Art of Falconry.* Edited and translated by Casey A. Wood and F. Marjorie Fyfe, Stanford, California: Stanford University Press, 1943.

Gies, Joseph and Frances. *Life in a Medieval City.* New York: Harper Perennial, 1981.

Goetze, Heinz. *Castel Del Monte: Geometric Marvel of the Middle Ages.* Germany: Prestel Publishers, 1998.

Sblendorio, Christopher. *The Falconer: A Story of Frederick II. of Hohenstaufen.* United States, AWSNA Publications, 2010. [for ages 6 and up]

ACKNOWLEDGEMENTS

First of all, I would like to thank Dee Marley of the Historical Fiction Company who has made this second edition of The Falconer's Apprentice possible. She also created the stunning new cover for the book. I would like to express my gratitude to the people who helped me in writing this book. First and foremost, I want to thank Stephen Roxburgh for his swift, perceptive, and constructive editorial input as much as for his kindness and encouragement. Troon Harrison of the Institute for Children's Literature read the first draft of this manuscript and with an unerring instinct for the big picture spurred me on in my attempts to fashion it into a finished product. I am grateful to Joan Giurdanella for her painstaking, thoughtful, and thorough work of copy-editing the manuscript. Andree White Snow read portions of the manuscript; her encouragement meant more than I can say. My brother Agostino contributed a wealth of literature that became an invaluable resource. On my bookshelf, I have some of the books about the thirteenth century that my brother Adrian loved as a boy. He more than anyone I know would have shared my delight in being able to work on this story. My father, Wolf Ulrich von Hassell, would have appreciated my attempt to delve into this historical period, providing gentle as well as sharp and incisive commentary on my misstatements and misinterpretations. One of the joys of this undertaking was that it became a framework for continuing conversations in my mind with those who are gone. So I dedicate this book to the wonderful and infinitely varied men in my life, both the living and the dead, but most of all, to my son, Vanya, who patiently put up with many badly cooked meals, burned meals, or sometimes no meals at all!

ABOUT THE BOOK

"That bird should be destroyed!"

Andreas stared at Ethelbert in shock. Blood from an angry- looking gash on the young lord's cheek dripped onto his embroidered tunic. Andreas clutched the handles of the basket containing the young peregrine. Perhaps this was a dream —Andreas, an apprentice falconer at Castle Kragenberg, cannot bear the thought of killing the young female falcon and smuggles her out of the castle. Soon he realizes that his own time there has come to an end, and he stows away, with the bird, in the cart of an itinerant trader, Richard of Brugge. So begins a series of adventures that lead him from an obscure castle in northern Germany to the farthest reaches of Frederick von Hohenstaufen's Holy Roman Empire, following a path dictated by the wily trader's mysterious mission.

Andreas continues to improve his falconry skills, but he also learns to pay attention to what is happening around him as he travels through areas fraught with political unrest. Eventually, Richard confides in Andreas, and they conspire to free Enzio, the eldest of the emperor's illegitimate sons, from imprisonment in Bologna.

The Falconer's Apprentice is a story of adventure and intrigue set in the intense social and political unrest of the Holy Roman Empire in the thirteenth century.

ABOUT THE AUTHOR

Malve von Hassell is a freelance writer, researcher, and translator. She holds a Ph.D. in anthropology from the New School for Social Research. Working as an independent scholar, she published *The Struggle for Eden: Community Gardens in New York City* (Bergin & Garvey 2002) and *Homesteading in New York City 1978-1993: The Divided Heart of Loisaida* (Bergin & Garvey 1996). She has also edited her grandfather Ulrich von Hassell's memoirs written in prison in 1944, *Der Kreis schließt sich - Aufzeichnungen aus der Haft 1944* (Propylaen Verlag 1994). She has taught at Queens College, Baruch College, Pace University, and Suffolk County Community College, while continuing her work as a translator and writer. She has published two children's picture books, *Tooth Fairy (Amazon KDP 2012/2020), and Turtle Crossing (Amazon KDP 2021)*, and her translation and annotation of a German children's classic by Tamara Ramsay, *Rennefarre: Dott's Wonderful Travels and Adventures* (Two Harbors Press, 2012). *The Falconer's Apprentice* (namelos, 2015) was her first historical fiction novel for young adults. She has published *Alina: A Song for the Telling* (BHC Press, 2020), set in Jerusalem in the time of the crusades, *The Amber Crane* (Odyssey Books, 2021), set in Germany in 1645 and 1945, and a biographical work about a woman coming of age in Nazi Germany, *Tapestry of My Mother's Life: Stories, Fragments, and Silences* (Next Chapter Publishing, 2021). She is working on a historical fiction trilogy featuring Adela of Normandy. To learn more about her work, visit her website at https://www.malvevonhassell.com